THE

RETRIBUTION

OF

LEVI BASS

A CLASSIC WESTERN STORY

G. MICHAEL HOPF

DEDICATION

TO THOSE WITH THE STRENGTH TO FORGIVE

"Forgiveness is the fragrance that the violet sheds on the heel that has crushed it."

- *Mark Twain*

CHAPTER ONE

JUNE 7, 1876

WICHITA, KANSAS

Levi didn't stand taller than five feet, but that didn't stop the ten-year-old from attempting to prevent his father, a drunkard, from taking what little money the family had to go gamble.

Leroy Bass wasn't just a man down on his luck, he was a man who had none. Everyone has met someone in their lives who was like Leroy. They were always the one person where things never quite worked out or bad things seemed to happen to. This was him. And today he had gotten into his head that he could beat Randall Pritchard, a notorious gunman and gambler. Leroy touted that he'd had a dream, a lucid one where he was sitting at the table across from Randall and was holding a king-high straight. He'd watched himself lay his hand down then look up to see Randall's eyes widen with shock, meaning that he, the son of a butcher, had beaten one of the best gamblers west of the Mississippi.

When he woke, he was filled with hope, but when would Leroy ever meet a man like Randall, he thought. He chalked it up to a fanciful dream, nothing more, then word spread a week later that Randall was in town, and of course he could be found at one of many tables.

Leroy took this as a sign that finally his ship had come in. He was meant to play Randall, and in order to do so he needed to use their life savings.

Levi's mother had been unable to stop Leroy from taking the money, but Levi wouldn't let up. He knew that without that money they'd starve or, worse, end up on the street again, a place he'd spent his sixth and seventh birthdays.

"No, Pa, please don't," Levi pleaded.

Having already drunk a bottle, Leroy was stumbling and mumbling, "Out of the damn way, boy."

"Please, Pa, that's all our money," Levi said, jumping in front of him.

Leroy stopped, looked at Levi, and barked, "Get out of my damn way, boy, or I'll smack you down!" He lifted his hand to strike but stopped short when he realized that Levi was ready to take the hit.

"You can hit me all you want, but I won't allow you to spend that money. We need it; we need it real bad," Levi said defiantly.

Howls and cheers erupted from the Crazy Eight Saloon and Gambling House.

Leroy looked towards the saloon, his eyes wide with excitement. "Step aside."

"No," Levi said, not moving.

Leroy shoved Levi to the ground and stepped over him.

Defiant, Levi jumped back up and once more blocked his father's path. "Please, Pa."

Leroy gritted his teeth and seethed. "Son, I don't want to hurt you, but I will."

"Pa, without that money we'll starve. We need it," Levi begged.

"I'm gonna win tonight, I know it," Leroy replied.

Levi placed his hands on his father's chest and cried, "Pa, you never win."

Anger swelled in Leroy when those words hit his ears. He snatched Levi by the throat and squeezed. "Shut your damn mouth, boy."

Clawing at his grip with both hands, Levi gasped, "Pa, you're choking me. I can't breathe."

Leroy leaned in so close that Levi could smell his sour breath. "Go home...now!" He shoved him aside; this time Levi landed in a mud puddle.

Covered in a combination of horse manure, urine and mud, Levi wiped his face and watched as Leroy marched on and into the saloon.

Inside, Leroy examined the bustling room. It was a familiar place; he normally found himself up at the bar, finishing off a bottle, or at one of the dozens of round tables, where he always seemed to lose. A large crowd in the far corner told him that was where he needed to be. He pushed his way through the swarm of people until he reached the table he was looking for. Sitting with his back to the wall was the man himself, Randall Pritchard. Like

in his dream he was wearing his black jacket and
burgundy vest; a gold chain dangled from the vest's left
pocket. His crisp white shirt was secured at the neck with
a matching burgundy cravat. Dangling from his teeth was
a slim cigar; his face was clean shaven, allowing the thick
scar that graced his cheek to be seen by all. He was proud
of that scar and would often talk about how he'd gotten
it. Leroy caught sight of the pearl-handled Colt Army he
wore on his hip, and chuckled, as Randall's pistol was
about as famous as he was.

"Mister, if you can beat a full house, queen high, the
pot is yours," Randall said, laying his hand down.

The remaining man playing against him threw his
cards on the table in anger and howled, "Damn it to hell!
How the hell do you do it? Huh?"

"Some say luck. I say skill," Randall replied, leaning
over and grabbing the pile of coins and cash. He shoved
it towards his side of the table and began to stack the
coins.

"You cleaned me out," the man said, pushing away
from the table and getting up.

Randall looked at the horde gathered and asked,
"Anyone else care to play?"

Leroy didn't reply. He was frozen in fear.

Looking at each person standing near the table,
Randall asked, "Want to play?" His question was quickly
answered by a no. Coming to Leroy, he asked, "Want to
play?"

Lost in the moment of it all, Leroy didn't answer.

"Mister! Do you want to play?" Randall said, his

voice louder.

Snapping out of his daze, Leroy recalled why he was there. "I'll play you."

"Take a seat," Randall said. Looking around again, he asked, "Anyone else care to join us?"

No one said yes.

"Looks like it's me and you. My name is Randall Pritchard, and whom might I be playing with?"

"Ah, my name is Leroy Bass. Um, I know who you are, heard a lot about you," Leroy said.

Chuckling, Randall smoothed out his thick black mustache and said, "Don't believe everything you hear."

"So you didn't shoot down the Barry brothers in Dodge last year?" Leroy asked, referring to two infamous outlaw brothers who were known for being gamblers and cutthroats.

"That, my friend, you can believe. I did shoot and kill them, but I have to say it was done in self-defense."

"And…"

"Shall we play?" Randall asked, growing impatient.

"Yes, of course," Leroy answered, pulling cash from his pocket. With his shaking hand, he placed it on the table.

"Two hundred, is that all you have?" Randall asked. He looked at the crumpled bills and then at Leroy. He could see he was drunk, and by his state of attire and hygiene, he knew he wasn't a well-to-do man and that the money on the table was more than likely all he had to his name. "Are you sure you want to play?"

"Yes, now deal," Leroy growled.

"I'm not so sure. Why do I feel that money there is all you have? If I take it, you'll be broke. Maybe you should reconsider."

"Just deal," Leroy barked.

Looking at everyone who surrounded them, Randall asked, "Should I play him?"

The crowd roared in unison, "Yes!"

"They say I should, but I think not. When people like you lose it all, you tend to lose it," Randall quipped.

Leroy slammed his fist on the table. "Deal the damn cards. And just so you know, I'm not aiming to lose, I'm aiming to beat you."

Smiling, Randall laughed. "You're a passionate man, aren't you?" He shuffled the deck and began to deal.

Leroy couldn't wait for the five cards to be dealt; he picked them up one by one as they came. As he gazed upon them, his dream appeared to be coming true, because in his hand was the queen of spades, ten of spades, nine of spades, two of hearts and six of clubs. In his dream the hand he won with was a straight flush, king high. Antsy to bet, he tossed twenty dollars into the center of the table.

"Oh yes, the ante," Randall said, tossing a twenty-dollar bill in as well. "Well, are we betting?"

Confusing his ante for a bet, Leroy put in another twenty. "I need two cards," he said, tossing two cards aside.

"I'll see that twenty and raise you fifty," Randall said, coming at him strong.

Leroy paused. He wanted to have faith in his dream,

but the fact of losing ninety dollars right away gnawed at him.

"Well?" Randall asked, his face stoic.

Commotion broke out behind Leroy. All turned to see Levi shove and push until he reached Leroy. "Pa, no, no, please, Pa, don't do this."

"Boy, I told you to go home," Leroy barked, his anger swelling.

"I take it this is your son?" Randall asked.

"It is and he's normally obedient," Leroy said, showing he was embarrassed by the disruption.

"What's his name?" Randall asked.

"Levi, my name is Levi, and please, mister, don't play my pa, please," Levi begged.

Randall roared in laughter.

Grabbing Levi by the collar, Leroy pulled him close. "You're making me look like a fool. Get outta here."

Randall placed his cards facedown and leaned back in his chair. "Come here, Levi."

Levi pulled away from Leroy and walked over to Randall. "Please, mister, don't play my pa."

"What's the problem?" Randall asked.

"That's all the money we have. If he loses it, we'll not have anything and, well, my pa, he don't work. If he loses this money we'll starve, you hear, we'll starve," Levi said pleading his case.

"Is this true?" Randall asked Leroy. "I suspected this was your story."

"The boy is lying. Don't listen to him. Now do you want to play or not?" Leroy snapped.

Randall cocked his head and said, "Of course I want to play, but I want to play men who should be playing, not ones who should be at home."

"Are you ridiculing me?" Leroy barked.

"Don't get jumpy. I'm looking out for you," Randall said.

"Mister, my pa has bad luck. He never wins this game," Levi said.

Leroy put his cards facedown, got up, and smacked Levi across the face. "Shut your mouth and go home to your mother."

Levi didn't fall this time. He recovered from the strike quickly, blood coursing down his chin, and gave Leroy an angry look. "I hate you."

"Do you make it a habit of hitting children?" Randall asked, focusing a hard stare on Leroy as he stiffened his spine.

Fully aware of Randall's reputation as a gunman, Leroy thought carefully about what he said next. He made his way back to his seat and sat. "I want to play, because the boy doesn't know what he's talking about. I'm going to beat you, Mr. Pritchard, with this hand." He tossed in the fifty and picked up his hand. "Now play or forfeit that money."

Randall looked at Levi and said, "Son, sometimes people need to be taught a lesson. Just know that I was willing to give him an out."

Levi didn't reply.

Randall dealt Leroy two cards and picked up two himself.

When Leroy gazed upon the two new cards, he about jumped out of his seat. This was his dream to a tee, for in his hand was a straight flush with spades, king high. He pushed the remaining money he had into the center of the table. "All in, one hundred and ten."

"Oh, Pa," Levi moaned.

Randall set his cards facedown and saw Leroy's wager. "Let's see what you have."

With a broad smile, Leroy laid his cards down.

The crowd gasped with many breaking out in chatter.

Fondly, Leroy looked around, feeling victorious. He was leaning across to grab the winnings when he was interrupted.

"Hold on," Randall said.

"I have a royal flush with spades, king high," Leroy said as if he couldn't be beat.

Randall set his cards down face up. "Royal flush with hearts...ace high."

The room erupted, many laughing at Leroy's expense while some shook their heads at how Randall seemed unbeatable.

Leroy's face went ashen; his jaw dropped open.

Randall dragged the cash towards himself. He gave Leroy a look and said, "Remember, I was willing to give you an out."

Sitting speechless, Leroy was in shock.

"Now who else wishes to play?" Randall asked.

"I was supposed to win...I was supposed to win," Leroy said under his breath.

"Clear out, and let some real players take a seat,"

Randall mocked Leroy.

Deflated emotionally and defeated spiritually, Leroy stood and walked out of the saloon.

Levi remained.

Randall said, "Best you go and take your pa home."

"I hate you," Levi said. "All you had to do was not play him, that's all you had to do. Now we're not going to be able to eat. We'll get tossed out onto the street."

"Like I said, boy, some people need to be taught a lesson," Randall said smugly.

"The only lesson I learned today is people like you are spiteful. All you had to do was not play him. You're responsible for us not eating," Levi barked.

"No, son, your father is responsible. He knew the stakes, yet he still played," Randall said, shuffling the cards. "And I gave him many outs; he chose to play."

"I hope you enjoy that money. By the looks of it, you will. That money will buy you a new pair of boots and a new suit with cuff links. To me that would have fed me and my mother," Levi snapped.

"I'm not sorry. He wanted to play, he knew the stakes, and still he played. Best you get on home and take care of your ma and pa," Randall said, putting his attention back on the game.

"I hate you," Levi said then marched off.

Watching him go, Randall laughed. "That boy has moxie."

***

Levi couldn't let go of his anger. All the way home he stewed over witnessing his father lose all their money and in no time. Never before had he told his father that he hated him. It was an emotion he now felt and one he feared would be with him for life.

He cleared the corner towards his house to hear his mother screaming, "How could you? We needed that."

"To hell with you!" Leroy screamed.

Levi knew what typically followed their verbal spats, so he raced to the house and through the door just in time to catch his father rearing back to hit his mother. "No," he said, grabbing Leroy's arm.

"Boy, you've been a pain in my ass all night. In fact, it's your fault I lost. You jinxed me," Leroy said.

"Leroy, how could you lose that money. We'll starve. We'll die," she groaned, her anger turning to sorrow. Tears flowed down her cheeks.

"Both of you shut up. I was supposed to win. I had a dream about it," Leroy declared.

"A dream? You had a dream?" she asked, mocking him.

"Don't you dare ridicule me. You need to show me respect," he fired back at her.

"Respect? I'm to show you respect? You're a drunk, a man who can't provide for his family. You're worthless, and now we could starve to death all because of you," she yelled.

Leroy's face went blank. He walked into the bedroom

then reappeared with a pistol in his hands. "I'm your husband. I'm the man of this house. You're to respect me!"

"Pa, what are you doing?" Levi asked.

"Does that gun make you feel like a man? You're going to need more than that 'cause you ain't one. You can't provide for us, and what you did tonight will put us in the grave," she spat.

"You're right, what I do tonight will," he said, cocking the pistol and pointing it at her chest.

"No, Pa," Levi hollered and ran at him.

It was too late. He pulled the trigger. The .44-caliber bullet blasted from the pistol and struck her in the chest. She reeled backwards, hitting the wall and sliding down. When she rolled onto the floor, she was dead.

Levi cried out.

Leroy cocked the pistol again, pivoted towards Levi, and shot him in the upper chest.

Levi toppled to the floor.

One last time he cocked it. Without hesitating or thinking twice, he placed the smoking muzzle against his throbbing temple and pulled the trigger.

CHAPTER TWO

JUNE 7, 1896 (TWENTY YEARS LATER)

PHOENIX, ARIZONA TERRITORY

L evi stared at his reflection in the mirror as he finished tying his necktie. He paused when he noticed the date on the calendar behind him. He turned and stared.

It was June 7 and exactly twenty years to the day since his father had killed his mother, wounded him, and then took his own life.

He'd since come to grips with that night, but not before living years with anger and guilt. He now forgave his father, something that wasn't easy to do. It had taken him a while, but with the help of his wife, Katherine, and his priest, Father McKenna, Levi was able to accept that his father was a deeply flawed man and that his actions were born from a deep-seated feeling of inadequacy and dependence on alcohol. Forgetting that night, though, proved harder. With the passage of two decades, he rarely thought of it, but when he did, it filled him with regret. His regret stemmed from his inability to stop his father as well as a guilt that Father McKenna described as survivor's guilt. There was one piece, one unsettled part of that night that haunted him. It was something he never mentioned, and that was Randall Pritchard's role in it. Although many would argue that Randall had nothing to do with his father's choice, Levi did still strongly feel that Randall had held all the proverbial cards that night and could have turned Leroy away, but he didn't; in fact, he taunted him upon winning the hand; to Levi, Randall was a guilty party that night.

A tap on the door tore him away from his painful thoughts. "Pa, breakfast is on the table," his son, Zeke, hollered.

"I'll be right down," Levi replied.

Zeke turned and barreled down the hall, a song sweetly coming from his lips. He turned and disappeared into the stairwell.

Levi smiled. He was a blessed man with a blessed life, and he owed it all to Katherine. The two had met twelve years ago while he was attending mass at St. John's Church. He hadn't been to church in many years, but something drew him that day. He wasn't sure what it was until he laid eyes on her. The second he saw her standing in the pew— her dark brown hair pulled up neatly into a tight bun, her milky white skin and light blue eyes—he was smitten. It took persistence, but eventually Katherine broke down and accepted an invitation from him to go have dinner together. Before long, they were engaged, then married. Nothing since that dreadful night had transformed him until they were husband and wife. For the first time in many years, he felt complete with a purpose and a plan.

Several years later Zeke was born; however, the pregnancy and delivery were difficult, almost resulting in Katherine dying.

That experience was enough for Levi to never want another child, leaving Zeke an only child. And when asked, Levi was fine with that decision. He tried to never be negative and strived to always find the positive in any situation.

Knowing he needed to get to breakfast, he grabbed his suit jacket, slipped it on, and smoothed out the creases. After one more viewing in the mirror, he headed out the door and down the stairs. Entering the dining room, he found Zeke sitting with his hands folded perfectly on top of the table.

"There you are," Zeke said with a jovial tone, his eyes widening with excitement even though he'd just seen Levi moments before.

"I pray I'm not late," Levi said, pulling his chair back. He sat down and asked, "Is your mother ready?"

"She is," Zeke said. "Ma, Pa is here!"

The door behind Levi opened and in stepped Katherine, two plates in her hands. She placed one in front of Levi and the other in front of Zeke. "Enjoy," she said, leaning over and giving Levi a quick kiss on the cheek. "Good morning, husband."

A broad smile creased Levi's face. He took her hand, looked up, and said, "Good morning, wife."

Zeke sat staring at his steaming food.

Katherine went back into the kitchen, grabbed her plate, and reappeared. She took a seat next to Levi and said, "Shall we pray?"

The three joined hands and bowed their heads.

Levi led them in a quick prayer. Upon finishing, he looked at his plate then to Katherine. "Breakfast looks magnificent."

Katherine scooted her eggs around on the plate, her anxiety showing through.

Noticing her nervousness, Levi set his fork down, reached over, and took her hand. "It's all going to work out, I assure you."

"I couldn't sleep last night. What if it doesn't?" she asked, her longing eyes staring at him with hopes he would assuage her.

"I've gotten assurances, you know this," Levi said.

"I'll trust you and God and stop worrying," she said, picking her fork back up. She dug into her eggs and began to eat.

Zeke smiled and said, "Pa, will we move right away?"

"I'll go ahead and find us a house; then I'll have you join me," he replied.

The three finished breakfast.

Looking at his watch, Levi shot up and said, "Look at the time. I need to rush." He sprinted for the door, stopping at the coat rack and bench.

Katherine came up just behind him and said, "Hold on, you can't rush out without this."

As Levi buckled his gun belt around his waist, he looked at the glimmering badge and smiled. "No, I can't leave without it."

She pinned it through the fabric of his vest and gently patted his chest. "I so look forward to pinning the marshal badge on your chest soon."

He looked deep into her eyes and said, "It will happen. I've waited patiently, and I'll get the job. Now please stop worrying."

"I said I was letting the worry go," she replied.

"Within a week or two, I won't be Sheriff Bass, I'll be Deputy United States Marshal Bass," he said with a broad smile stretched across his face.

"That has a nice ring to it," she said, leaning in and giving him a kiss on the lips.

He returned the kiss, smiled and said, "I'll see you tonight, and please, don't worry, nothing will happen. I've got the job."

DODGE CITY, KANSAS

Randall slipped on his shirt and buttoned it, his mind spinning with what the doctor would tell him. He had a good idea, but hearing it would provide him a bit of closure to what had been a month of pain and confusion.

The door opened and in stepped Dr. Graham. "Mr. Pritchard, if you need more time to dress—"

"Doc, you think I'm a modest person? Please come on in and give me the bad news," Randall barked.

Graham approached Randall, stopping feet from him. "How do you know it's bad news?"

"I've been coughing up blood for a straight month,

and I can barely wake up these days due to the fatigue and malaise; I'm not fool enough to think this is merely a cold that will pass."

"You have throat cancer for sure by the lumps I see at the back of your throat; that's what's been causing you difficulty with swallowing. The coughing up blood tells me it's spread to your lungs, and it could be elsewhere too."

Randall cleared his throat, which he did often now, looked squarely at Graham, and asked, "How long do I have?"

"Hard to tell, could be weeks, but I've seen people last longer. If I were you, Mr. Pritchard, I would consider tying up any loose ends and managing what affairs you have while you can," Graham replied.

"How will it go?" Randall asked.

"Things will only get worse. The fatigue and pain will worsen, then…"

Waving his hand, Randall said, "Never mind, forget I asked." He slipped his coat on and donned his wide-brimmed hat. "How much?"

"Twenty-eight dollars," Graham said.

Randall pulled out his wallet, pulled several bills out, and tossed them on a table. "Keep the change and, Doc, thank you for seeing me on such short notice."

Graham pocketed the cash and said, "I'm sorry, Mr. Pritchard."

"I'm sorry too," Randall said, walking to the door.

"Do you have family?"

"None that want to see me," Randall said, laughing.

"Now is the time to try to make amends, if that's

possible," Graham said.

Randall nodded, as he'd been thinking often of seeing his only daughter. It had been fifteen years since he'd seen her last, but maybe if she knew he was dying, she'd want to rekindle their relationship.

"Where is this family?" Graham asked.

"Phoenix."

"Will you take my advice and go? Trust me when I say that the only regret a dying man has on his deathbed is not being with family," Graham said.

"I think I will. I've never seen the desert; why not before I die?" Randall said.

"You take care of yourself," Graham said.

Randall tipped his hat, opened the door, and exited. The bustling of the street in front of him tore him away from his worries. He loved the excitement of Dodge City, but especially enjoyed the gambling halls. They were what had brought him there years before. The city brought him an endless stream of novice young gamblers all hoping they'd be the one to take him down, and each time he proved them wrong. His notorious reputation brought him many enemies, most of whom tried to take him out with a pistol after failing at the card table, but all failed there too. His pursuit of winnings had bestowed on him many lifetimes of wealth, but now that he was close to death, all he wanted was connection, and the only place he'd be able to find that was in Phoenix with his daughter, Savannah.

But before he'd take that trip, he first needed to quench his thirst for gambling. He strutted across the street and walked into the Daisy, a saloon and gambling hall. He looked around at the mostly filled tables, searching for the one. Upon spotting it, he marched over, pulled out a wad of cash, and tossed it on the table. "Who wants to play some high stakes?"

***

A crowd had gathered around the table, not an unlikely event when Randall was playing. As usual, a large pile of coins and cash lay in the center of the table, with only one man left playing against him.

"I've been sitting here trying to get an idea of why you look familiar, and now I know," the man across from Randall said, his playing cards in his hand.

"I, for the life of me, don't know you, sir," Randall snorted.

"You're Randall Pritchard, the famous gambler and gunman," the man said.

"Guilty as charged," Randall said.

"I knew it, I told you it was him," the man said, slapping a man to his right.

"Are you going to call my raise or just talk?" Randall asked.

"Seeing that my hand is nearly impossible to beat, I'll see you and raise you a hundred," the man said, pushing the correct amount of cash forward.

Not hesitating, Randall saw his bet and raised it again. "How about another three hundred?"

The man paused and gave his friend a quick look.

"Don't look to him. You're playing me, not him,"

Randall growled.

"Are you sayin' I'm cheatin'?" the man asked, his tone signaling he didn't like the derogatory comment.

"I'm saying, sir, that we're playing cards, your friend isn't, so don't look to him for advice or assurance. Now are you going to see my bet or fold?" Randall asked.

The man gulped, a bead of sweat forming on his brow.

Spotting the perspiration, Randall knew he had him. The man's hand was either a bluff or he had just lost confidence in it.

"I'm waiting," Randall said. "See my raise or fold."

The man's concerned look vanished and was quickly replaced by joy. With a broad smile he answered, "I'll see that additional three hundred and go higher another two hundred."

Randall chuckled. He picked up a small stack of coins and tossed it in. "There, now let's see this hand you think is so good."

"Full house, kings over eights," the man said, laying his hand down.

"Now that is a good hand, a very good hand," Randall said.

The crowd around began to chatter and grow louder.

"Well, did I get ya? Huh?" the man asked Randall.

"That really is a good hand, but not a great one like this," Randall said, setting his cards down. "Full house, aces over jacks."

The man gritted his teeth and seethed in anger. "That's a bunch of crap. I had you beat."

"Like I said, mister, that was a good hand, but I had a

great hand; today is not your day," Randall said, reaching out and sliding the winnings towards himself.

"You cheated, you did," the man barked.

Gasps and silent cross talk erupted when the accusation was made.

Randall stopped what he was doing, leaned back in his chair, and asked, "You're calling me a cheater?"

"I am. I've heard about you. They say you either have a pact with the devil, which gives you incredible luck, or you cheat. I think you cheat," the man growled, his right hand sliding slowly towards his hip.

"A pact with the devil? Now that would be something else, but the thing is…" Randall said then paused as he pulled his pearl-handled Colt from his holster, cocked it and fired. The round struck the man in the chest. Randall cocked it again and shot the man. This time the bullet struck him in the neck.

The man choked as blood poured down his windpipe. He clutched the wound and toppled out of the chair.

Randall stood, cocked the pistol again, and leveled it at the man's head. "But the thing is, I don't need to cheat or make a pact with the devil, I'm just that good." He pulled the trigger and ended the man's life. With the deed done, Randall twirled the pistol on his finger and promptly holstered it. He scanned the room, looking for the man's friend. Spotting him near the back, he said, "Don't think about doing something stupid, or I'll put a round in you too."

The man's friend leered at Randall then bolted out of the saloon.

Randall cried out, "If anyone else wants to cross me or call me a cheater, step up now and we'll deal with it proper!"

The room was silent.

"Very well then," Randall said. He collected his winnings and went to the bar.

A bearded man greeted him from behind the bar, an apron wrapped around his waist. "What can I get you?"

"You the owner of this establishment?" Randall asked.

"I am," the man replied. His name was Butch, and he often went by the nickname Bearded Butch, due to his long thick beard, which hung down to the center of his chest.

Randall tossed twenty dollars in coins on the bar and said, "That's for the mess."

Butch snatched the coins and pocketed them. "We're good now."

Tipping his hat, Randall said, "Have a good night." He strolled out of the Daisy as he had walked in, his head held high.

CHAPTER THREE

JUNE 12, 1896

PHOENIX, ARIZONA TERRITORY

L evi lifted his head when the door of his office opened, and in stepped the postman. "Are you here to see me?"

"I am, Sheriff," the postman answered. He walked over and held a single letter in his hand.

Levi took it and immediately looked for the return address. When he saw it was from Prescott, he knew who sent it and what it was about. He tore it open and unfolded the letter. Reading hastily, he got to the part where it informed him he'd been chosen to be the next deputy United States marshal. "It's official."

"It looks like good news," the postman said, smiling.

Not noticing he was still standing there, Levi said, "It is. Now unless I can help you with anything else, please show yourself out."

"Of course, take care and have a good day, Sheriff," the postman said, tipping his hat before exiting the office.

Levi sprang to his feet and bolted for the door, but before he could reach it, his deputy, a man by the name of Ernest Thompson, swept in. "Sheriff, we've got a big-name gunslinger who just arrived in town."

"A gunslinger? Are there any more of them these days?" Levi joked.

"Seriously, Sheriff, he just checked into the Rising Sun Hotel," Thompson said.

"Who is this notorious gunslinger?" Levi asked.

"It's Randall Pritchard," Thompson replied.

Levi's face turned ashen.

Noticing his complexion had changed, Thompson said, "Sheriff, you don't look well."

As Levi turned around and walked back to his desk, his mind spun. *How is it that he's here? Why is he here? What should I do about it? Should I seek justice?*

"Sheriff, is everything alright?" Thompson said, walking farther into the office and towards Levi.

"I'm fine, I, um," he replied. Knowing he needed to get control of his emotions, he stood upright, cleared his throat, and continued, "Do you know what Randall Pritchard is doing here?"

"No idea," Thompson answered.

"Go find out. See if he's just passing through or if he means to stay awhile," Levi said, his back still facing Thompson.

"Sure thing, Sheriff," Thompson said and bolted out of the office as fast as he'd arrived.

When the door shut, Levi gasped. He loosened his tie and put all of his weight against the desk to support him, as his legs felt wobbly. "Get ahold of yourself, Levi," he said out loud. Seeing the letter in his hand, he thought about going home to tell Katherine but stopped short of doing so until he could get his emotions under control. He walked back around his desk and plopped into the chair. Pressing his eyes closed, he focused on his breathing and kept questioning why Randall was in town and if he should confront the man he blamed for that night.

DODGE CITY, KANSAS

Silvester Hoffman, aka Fester, looked down on the unmarked grave that held his brother's remains. Anger began to well up inside him. It was the first time he'd experienced it since hearing about Ronald's murder. He had rushed from Michigan with hopes he could bring Ronald back to Lansing so he could be buried alongside his family.

Fester cleared his throat and ordered, "Dig him up."

The two young laborers, Jim and Gavin, whom he'd contracted, began digging.

With each shovel full of dirt, Fester's anger grew.

Within minutes one of the men's shovels hit the wood top of the casket.

"They didn't even have the decency to bury him six feet." Fester scowled.

"Sir, maybe it's best you go to the saloon and wait for us to finish," Gavin said as he gave Fester a concerned look.

"Just do your job and get the casket out of the

26

ground," Fester barked.

Gavin went back to work. In no time they had the casket out of the grave and on the back of a wagon. "Where do you want us to take it?" Gavin asked.

"Open it up," Fester said, walking up to the casket. He rubbed his hand alongside the dirt-caked wood and again said, "Open it up. I want to see him."

"Sir, is that such a good idea? He was buried four or five days ago," Gavin said.

Jim blurted out with a devilish smile, "He's gonna be ripe."

Fester shot him a harsh look and exclaimed, "I hear you make another derogatory comment about my brother and I'll put you in a casket." He pulled his overcoat aside and placed his hand on the back strap of his pistol.

Jim gulped, regret and fear gripping his pudgy face.

Doing as they were told, the men pried open the lid of the casket and set it aside. Just as Jim had predicted, Ronald was ripe. The stench of rotting flesh surrounded them all.

Unfazed by the pungent odor, Fester gazed upon the bloated body of Ronald, his face swollen and black from pooled blood. The wound on his neck and in the head clearly visible. "Who did this to you?"

"Randall Pritchard did that to him. Yep, I was there when it happened," Jim said.

Fester turned to Jim and asked, "You know who murdered my brother?"

"I wouldn't call it murder. From my vantage point—" Jim said before being interrupted by Gavin as he elbowed him in his side.

"Damn it, Jim, be sensitive to the gentleman here. This is his brother," Gavin said.

"But it wasn't murder," Jim replied, giving Gavin a look of shock that he'd been corrected.

"Where can I find the man who murdered my brother?" Fester asked.

"Sir, I hope you're not thinking of going after him. He's a notorious gunslinger, a real gunman," Gavin said.

"I once heard he shot six men down in less than twelve seconds," Jim howled.

Fester's anger had reached its high; he ripped his pistol from its holster and stuck it under Jim's chin. "I suggest you get your fat mouth shut."

"Listen, mister, we're just here to help you dig up and deliver your brother's casket. We don't want any trouble," Gavin said.

"Then tell your fat friend to keep his opinions to himself," Fester warned.

"I heard he left town. Some say he's sick, that he has the lung disease," Jim said slowly, his arms raised.

"Where did he go?" Fester asked.

"Out west somewhere, I don't rightly know," Jim replied.

"Me either," Gavin said.

Fester uncocked the pistol and holstered it. "Put the lid back on and deliver it to the undertaker."

"But he's already been to the undertaker," Jim said.

"The undertaker didn't do a good job. He needs to clean him up before I ship him back. Now do as I say," Fester barked.

The men nodded. They secured the lid, raised the tailgate, and climbed onto the wagon.

"Where did you say he was murdered?" Fester asked.

"The Daisy, he was playing poker there when he was shot down," Gavin answered before Jim could open his mouth.

Climbing onto his horse, Fester pulled the reins and sprinted off towards the Daisy. There he hoped to get more information on that night and about the man who had killed Ronald.

PHOENIX, ARIZONA TERRITORY

Randall had woken to a coughing fit, leaving him further fatigued than he already was, but his determination got him out of bed.

He made his way down to the dining room after getting dressed, to find the space full of fellow hotel guests.

A waiter approached and asked, "Shall I set you a table?"

"Yes," Randall replied.

"Will anyone else be joining you?" the waiter asked.

"Just me," Randall said, a common phrase for him.

"Very well, right this way, sir," the waiter said as he navigated through the maze of tables and set him up at a small round table near the window. "Here you go. Shall I pour you a coffee?"

"Yes," Randall replied, taking a seat.

The waiter rushed off.

Randall peered out the window and marveled at the

throng of people on the street. Where were they all going? What were they doing?

The waiter reappeared and set down as steaming cup of coffee. "Have you looked at our menu yet?"

"Bacon and two eggs, firm yolks, and a piece of toast," Randall said.

The waiter turned to leave but was stopped when Randall added to his order.

"Bring two pieces of toast and a side of jam," Randall said. He had a sweet tooth, it was something he fought over the years, but in his current condition, he had decided to just enjoy himself.

"What kind? We have—"

Cutting him off, Randall replied, "Surprise me."

"Very well, sir," the waiter said and hurried away.

He picked up the coffee and sipped. When he lifted his gaze, he saw a middle-aged woman staring at him. He gave her a smile, which she returned in kind. She too was sitting alone. Unconcerned what people would think, he got up and approached her. "Are you dining alone?"

"I am," she answered sweetly.

He estimated she was closer to fifty than forty, still young for a man of sixty-three. "Mind if I join you?"

"You may. That would be nice," she said.

He brought his cup of coffee to the table and sat.

Leaning in, she said, "Sitting alone in a restaurant always makes me feel self-conscious."

"It's normal for me," he said.

"You prefer that?" she asked.

He thought for a moment then replied, "I suppose I

do. My life just ended up that way."

"No one's life ends up randomly. We all get what we put in," she said, picking up her hot tea and sipping.

"You're right, it isn't random. I like being alone," he said.

"Except today?" she asked.

He smiled and said, "Except now, of course. I consider it my duty to sit here."

She placed her cup of tea back on the table and laughed. "Duty? My, aren't we chivalrous?"

Sitting tall in the chair, he said, "I do fashion myself after the knights of old."

The waiter returned and placed his food on the table. He glanced to the woman and asked, "Have you chosen what you'll have, ma'am?"

"I'm quite fine with my tea," she answered.

Looking at his food then to her, Randall said, "I don't want to eat alone. Please order something."

"I'm quite fine. I don't have much of an appetite," she said.

"Are you sure?"

She peeked at his plate and asked, "Are those eggs cooked runny or firm?"

"Slightly firm," he replied.

"That's how I like them," she said.

He promptly raised his hand and whistled loudly.

Their waiter turned towards them.

"A plate, and hurry," Randall shouted.

"Oh no, I'm really not hungry," she said, feeling awkward.

The waiter returned with a plate.

Randall snatched it, picked up one of the eggs, and placed it on the plate. He set a single piece of bacon next to it along with one of the slices of toast. He reached across the table and set it in front of her. "Bon appétit."

She laughed and asked, "You speak French?"

"Yes, if you consider only knowing those two words counts."

"You shouldn't have done that," she said, feeling embarrassed.

"I won't dine alone, and I believe you didn't want to order because you were sitting by yourself."

"Is that what you think?" she asked, curious about the comment.

"I'm good at reading people. I can look across any table and within minutes know what someone is thinking or feeling," Randall said confidently.

Cocking her head in amazement at his claim, she asked, "So you're a clairvoyant?"

"I'm not sure what that word means, but if it's a compliment, I'll take it." He laughed.

She laughed in response.

"Now can we both dig in? I'm hungry," he said.

Picking up her silverware, she replied, "Yes, let's eat." She carved off a piece of egg white and yolk and placed it in her mouth. After swallowing, she said, "That is good, perfectly cooked."

"It sure is," he replied.

"I feel so rude. I'm enjoying part of your breakfast and your company, and I don't even know your name," she said.

"I'm the rude one," he said, placing his utensils down. Extending his hand across the table, he continued, "The name is Randall Pritchard, ma'am."

"Nice to meet you, Randall Pritchard. My name is Mrs. Jane Tyne."

"What brings you to Phoenix?" he asked, returning to his food.

"Mr. Pritchard—"

Interrupting her, he said, "Call me Randall."

Nodding, she continued, "I wouldn't normally do this, but I came here to die."

Randall started to cough as he almost choked on his food. Shocked by her blunt reply, he asked, "Die? Do you jest?"

"Unfortunately I don't. My doctor told me the dry desert air would be best for my lungs."

"You have consumption?" he asked.

"I do," she answered, her jovial expression from before melting away to one of sadness.

"I'm sorry to hear that."

The two sat unmoving and silent for a moment before Randall shattered it with a chuckle.

Confused by his laughter, she asked, "Please share with me what is humorous. I could so use some amusement."

"I can assure you, my laughter isn't born from your situation. I laugh because I too am here to die," he confided.

Her mouth dropped open. "You are?"

"I am, but it's not your ailment. I have cancer and my days are short, at least that's what the doctor told me a week ago," Randall explained.

"You look as fit as a fiddle," she said.

"I don't always feel that way." He laughed.

Jane smiled sweetly and looked away from him.

"What's the look for?" he asked.

Lifting her head, she asked, "I thought you could read people?"

"I can, I just want you to say it," he flirted.

"Go ahead, try to guess," she said.

Leaning back in his chair, he smoothed out his long gray mustache and answered, "You're happy to have met someone you can relate to."

Her eyes widened with awe.

"I'm right, aren't I?"

"You are. It's been so long since I've had a connection with someone—"

Interrupting her, he asked, "We have a connection?"

Keeping her word to be as honest as she could be in the final days of her life, she answered, "We do. You are a man who likes to be alone, yet you came to want my company. Also, I didn't want to come downstairs this morning because a melancholy state has infected me since I woke, but I told myself that today something would happen that would put a smile on my face, so I forced myself to come here. And look what happened. You found company and I found my smile; we were meant to meet."

"I can't offer a rebuttal to that. I'm glad I was of value to make such a pretty face more beautiful by putting a smile on it. You, my dear, are correct too; I was in need of company. It's a feeling I haven't felt in...well, I don't think I've ever felt it."

"It changed when you found out you were dying, didn't it?" she asked.

"It did," he replied. He thought for a brief moment and continued, "Where is Mr. Tyne?"

"My dear husband died years ago. I'm a widow," she answered.

"And children?"

"All grown, two boys, they left home a while ago to pursue their fortunes in Alaska gold country," she said.

"Do they know about your condition?" he asked, placing his elbows on the table and leaning in closer.

She fiddled with the seam on her skirt, hesitant to answer.

"Did I ask something inappropriate?" he asked, genuinely concerned.

"I haven't told them. They're so happy off in the wilds of the north country. If I told them, they'd drop everything and come to be by my side."

"Don't you want that?"

"No, I don't. Of course I'd love to see them, but not like this, not dying. I don't want their last memory of me to be sickly and bedridden. I don't want them to miss out on striking their fortune because they needed to come sit by my side only to watch me die slowly."

"You know something, Mrs. Tyne, that's an honorable thing you're doing, if you ask me."

"You don't judge me?"

"Judge you? Ha, I applaud you. You're letting your boys be men. You're also not worrying them. You're thinking about their futures."

"That's exactly how I look at it. If they came to be by my side, they'd have to be gone for months and months. That would put their endeavors at risk. I want them to be successful, to find wealth. Money was something we never had while they were growing up. Those boys have strong minds and will become very successful if left to their own devices. I won't get in their way, no, I won't."

Randall again smiled and said, "You're not only honorable but wise, Mrs. Tyne."

"If I'm to call you Randall, I insist you call me Jane, please," she said.

Randall reached across the table again, his hand open.

She placed her hand in his.

Shaking her hand gingerly, he said, "Jane, it's my pleasure to meet you."

DODGE CITY, KANSAS

Fester took the glass of whiskey sitting in front of him and tossed it back.

"Where are you from, mister? I don't recognize you," Butch, the owner of the Daisy asked, wiping a shot glass clean.

"Michigan, Lansing, Michigan," Fester answered, shoving the empty glass forward.

Butch promptly filled the glass and asked, "You a gambler?"

"No, I despise gambling, but I despise something else more," Fester replied, picking up the glass and throwing it back as quickly as the first.

"And what's that, friend?" Butch asked.

"Gamblers," Fester barked loudly.

Several curious heads turned towards him.

"Then you came to the wrong place. Just behind you sit about two dozen gamblers," Butch said, nodding towards the tables over Fester's shoulder.

"Fill it," Fester said, pushing the glass towards Butch.

Obliging, Butch pulled the cork on the bottle and filled the glass. He gave Fester a smirk and asked, "If it's not gambling, what else brings you from Michigan?"

"To pick up my brother."

"Oh, where is he?"

"He's sittin' in a casket at the undertaker's," Fester answered.

Butch's expression changed to shock. "My condolences."

"I don't want your condolences, I want answers," Fester snapped.

"Not sure if I can help," Butch said as he slowly stepped away from Fester.

"Randall Pritchard," Fester said.

Hearing the name, Butch paused. "What about him?"

"Where can I find him?" Fester asked, pouring the contents of the shot glass down his throat. He slammed the glass on the bar, but this time he grabbed the bottle himself and filled his empty glass.

"I don't know," Butch replied. "I don't keep tabs on

men like him. They tend to like their privacy."

Fester flipped open his trench coat enough for Butch to see his pistol.

"I don't respond to threats, and if you pull that, someone else will gun you down for sure," Butch said, motioning with his head towards someone behind Fester.

Looking over his shoulder, Fester saw two men, their pistols in their hands and their eyes glued to him. "Fair enough."

"If you're here to make trouble, I suggest you leave walking before you leave being dragged out," Butch said.

Fester pulled out a twenty-dollar coin and flipped it onto the wet bar. It clanged when it hit and spun for a second before resting. "Will this help, then?"

Butch reluctantly stepped forward. He reached for the coin, but Fester grabbed his hand. He turned it over and place the coin in his open palm.

"Where can I find Randall Pritchard?" Fester asked.

"He headed out west," Butch replied.

"Where?"

"Arizona."

"That's a big territory. Where in Arizona can I find that murdering son of a bitch?" Fester growled.

"He'll kill me if he finds out I told you," Butch said.

"The man murdered my brother in here not a week ago. I'm aiming to get revenge, so tell me where," Fester said.

"Was that your brother?" Butch asked.

"It was my little brother, Ronald. He was a good man, minus his taste for gambling, but I've forgiven him. What

I can't forgive is the man who gunned him down and those willing to help him."

"Phoenix, he went to Phoenix," Butch blurted out.

"Are you sure?" Fester asked.

"Randall is a smart and savvy man, but he made the mistake of hiring Doc Graham; he talks more than a drunk Irishman. He told me the other night that Pritchard is dying from cancer, has it real bad. Told him to go see what family he has to make amends. He said before he left his office that Pritchard told him he was headed out west to Phoenix, that he'd never seen the desert before and that he should before he died."

Fester released Butch's hand.

"Now that's all I know," Butch said.

Tossing another twenty-dollar coin on the bar, Fester said, "That's for the bottle and for a room for the night."

Butch picked up the second coin and pocketed it. "Take room number six."

Fester tipped his hat and strutted off.

"Mister, you really aren't fool enough to go after Randall Pritchard, are ya?" Butch asked.

Fester stopped and turned around. "I will be heading west, and when I see Randall Pritchard, I'll be putting a round in between his damn eyes."

"You do know many men have tried and failed?"

"I pay no heed to such talk," Fester said.

"It'll be your funeral," Butch said.

Ignoring Butch's latest comment, Fester asked, "One other thing, barkeep, where's the closest telegraph office?"

PHOENIX, ARIZONA TERRITORY

Savannah Stone clasped her hands tightly and squeezed. She was finding it difficult to look Mr. Sullivan, the bank manager, in the eyes. She felt if she did for a prolonged period of time, he'd see just how much she hated him.

"Mrs. Stone, I know it might seem very unfair, but a widow is responsible for her husband's debts," Sullivan said.

"I didn't know he mortgaged the house; he never told me. And why, why did he do it?" she asked.

Savannah was recently widowed, her husband dying unexpectedly. He'd been found along the road from Scottsdale to Phoenix within the Phoenix city limits, his head showing blunt-force trauma to the temple. It had been determined by Marshal Clark that he'd fallen from his horse and hit his head on a rock after a night of drinking.

"Mrs. Stone, we don't ask our customers that sort of information. He needed the monies and used your house and land as collateral. As you can see here, this is the mortgage contract and the lien we have against the property," Sullivan said, sliding the documents across his desk for her to review.

"I don't need to see those. His debt is his debt; I don't think it's fair."

"Mrs. Sullivan, that's not how this works. We gave him money, a lot of it. We collateralized it by placing a lien against the house and land. If you cannot make payments, then we will be forced to foreclose and take the house and land."

Tears welled in her eyes. "My husband isn't dead a month and you now are threatening to take my house and land?"

"No, no, no, that is not what I'm doing, Mrs. Stone. I'm merely informing you of the arrangement we have with you."

"It's not my arrangement, it's the arrangement you made with my dead husband. He's gone and that ends this."

"Mrs. Stone, please understand, that is not how this works, and any court will back up our claim to your house and land if you fail to make your payments," Sullivan insisted in a tempered tone. He could clearly see she was distraught, and didn't want to cause her further upset.

"You're going to take me to court, a widow?"

"The contract we had with your husband is a legal document. The law is one hundred percent behind us on this, I'm sorry. I wish I could tell you something else, but I'm simply telling you that you are obligated to keep making the payments," Sullivan said.

Savannah grunted and asked, "What did he do with the money you gave him?"

"I don't know."

"This is a bank, isn't it? Did he open an account here?"

"No, he didn't. I wish he had; then you could have access to those funds," Sullivan said, sympathizing with her dilemma.

"My husband mortgages the house and land, hides the money, dies, and I'm responsible for paying the payment, yet I have no employment, no way of earning money?"

"I can talk to the board and plead your case. Maybe we can give you more time to make payments," Sullivan said.

"Will you do that?" she asked.

"I will, but I make no guarantees."

A single tear streaked down her cheek. She quickly wiped it away. Standing up to leave, she said, "Thank you for your time, Mr. Sullivan. I'll be back at the end of the week to get the answer from the board."

Sullivan got to his feet and extended his hand.

She ignored his gesture and turned to leave. She wasn't being rude; she didn't want to start crying in front of him.

"Good day, Mrs. Stone," Sullivan said, not taking offense to her snub.

She didn't reply. She exited the bank and stood on the wooden walkway. Before her was the busy intersection of Washington and Maricopa Streets. Directly across from that was the center square of town. Directly in the middle stood a flagpole with Old Glory flying high. She watched as the gentle breeze lapped the sides of the flag. It brought a memory back of her first time there. She and Brant had just moved from Tucson three months before. He had hopes for opening a blacksmith shop, but first his goal was to get the house and barn fixed up. Seven weeks later he was dead. Now she found herself alone in a city she didn't know and broke with the threat of foreclosure looming over her. She looked left then right; she didn't even know where to go next. Her heart thumped in her chest at the proposal of losing all they had both worked so hard to achieve. The move to Phoenix was to be a fresh start, a break for them. He'd run a successful blacksmith shop in Tucson but sold it, took the proceeds, and bought the land and house she was in now. What she couldn't come to grips with was wondering what he had been doing behind her back. Where was the money he'd taken out against the house and land? Why did he lie to her? He would go out once a week and drink with some new friends he'd become acquainted with, but she didn't even know their names or where he went on those nights. Filled with so many questions that could never be truly answered, she took a step, then another until she was standing in front of her wagon. If life had taught her one thing, it was to never quit. She would need to find employment and quickly, but where would she find it? She climbed onto the wagon, took the reins, and headed home; there she'd find a way, there she'd be able to figure it all out.

***

Thompson entered the sheriff's office to find it engulfed in darkness. He made his way to a lantern on his desk and lit it. When the light chased the dark away, he jumped when he saw Levi sitting in his chair, motionless and silent. "Gosh darn it, Sheriff, you scared me."

Levi didn't reply; he sat, eyes wide open, staring at his desk.

Cautiously, Thompson approached. "Sheriff, are you well?"

"Did you find out anything?" Levi asked, finally speaking up.

"About Randall Pritchard?"

"Yes, Thompson, about Randall Pritchard," Levi snarled.

"Not much more than I knew this morning. He's staying down the street, and he was seen earlier in the day in the company of a woman by the name of Jane Tyne. Nothing more than that. He's not been to any gambling halls, nor has he gone anywhere except Montgomery's General Store. There he purchased some tobacco, a newspaper and some licorice."

"Nothing else?" Levi asked.

"No, Sheriff, that's it. What would you like me to do?" Thompson asked.

"Never mind, I'll find out myself," Levi said, jumping to his feet.

"Sheriff, are you sure you're well?" Thompson asked.

"I'm fine, Deputy, just fine," Levi said.

"Are you headed home?" Thompson asked.

"No, Deputy Thompson, I'm not headed home yet. I'm going to go find out what you couldn't," Levi said.

"Sheriff?"

Levi stopped and turned.

"What's going on? As soon as I told you about Randall Pritchard, you started acting odd. I know he doesn't have a warrant out for him in any state or territory. So why the odd behavior and curiosity concerning him?"

"It's personal," Levi answered.

Sensing something could go wrong, Thompson said, "Sheriff, you're not about to do something you'll regret, are you?"

"Deputy Thompson, all you need to know is I'm the sheriff and you're not. I needed to know some information concerning Randall Pritchard and you couldn't get it, so I'll go find out myself," Levi stated firmly.

"How about I come with you?" Thompson said, stepping towards the door.

"You stay here," Levi said before changing his mind. "Actually, go to my house and tell Katherine I'll be late tonight. Don't tell her why, and whatever you do, do not mention Randall Pritchard."

"Got it. Tell her you'll be late and…"

"Do not mention Randall Pritchard."

"Right, do not mention him, but why?" Thompson asked, curious as to what on earth could be troubling Levi. He had always known him as a calm and decisive man. His actions were very much out of character.

"It's personal, I said, and Katherine would get very upset, so do not upset her," Levi growled.

"I won't, Sheriff, I promise," Thompson said, grabbing his hat.

"And when you're done that, come back to the office," Levi ordered.

"Yes, Sheriff," Thompson said.

"And, Deputy, do not mention Pritchard to my wife," Levi once more reiterated.

"I won't, Sheriff, you have my word," Thompson said, rushing off.

***

Levi entered the Rising Sun Hotel and marched up to the front desk.

"Good evening, Sheriff," Dale said.

"What room is Randall Pritchard in?" Levi asked.

"Now, Sheriff, we can't give out a guest's room number, you should know this," Dale said.

"What room? I need to go see him, it's urgent," Levi said, clarifying his previous question.

"Well, if you need to see Mr. Pritchard, he's just in there," Dale said, pointing towards the dining hall.

Levi spun around and looked.

The dining hall was full of patrons, many eating, but one table had four people sitting at it playing cards. No doubt that was where Randall was.

Levi took a few steps but paused when he began to reconsider what he was about to do. He'd spent the entire day sitting and thinking. He had always told himself that he'd left his life in Kansas behind him, including Randall Pritchard, but if they ever crossed paths, then he'd kill him. Now here he was feet from the man who was responsible for his parents' demise. When he left the sheriff's office, he was determined to exact revenge. It was so easy, all he needed to do now was walk up without saying a word, pull his Colt, and put a bullet in his head.

Gathering his determination to do what he'd sworn he'd do, he began his march toward Randall again.

A hand reached from behind Levi, grabbed him by the shoulder, and spun him around. "Sheriff Bass, what in the hell are you doing in here?"

Levi was startled. He looked at Gus Clark, the town marshal, and said, "Oh, hello, Marshal."

"Son, you look out of sorts. Are you doing alright?" Clark asked.

"I was, um, I was just heading to see what the commotion was about," Levi said, pointing towards Randall and the small group that had gathered around his table.

"Oh, you heard, huh? Pritchard arrived yesterday. He and I go way back, from when I was a deputy sheriff in Manhattan, Kansas."

"You know him?" Levi asked, shocked.

"I sure do. Sorta feels odd now. He's become quite famous," Clark said, pulling his trousers up around his rotund belly.

"More notorious than famous," Levi snorted.

"Isn't that the same thing?" Clark said.

"No, notorious means…never mind," Levi said, shaking his head. He was stunned by Clark's presence and his relation to Randall.

"Come, let me introduce you," Clark said, draping his arm over Levi's shoulder and ushering him into the room. "Randall, I want you to meet the sheriff of Maricopa County, Levi Bass."

Randall looked up from his hand and said, "Sheriff, nice to make your acquaintance."

Levi gritted his teeth and said, "Mr. Pritchard, what's a man of your reputation doing in Phoenix?"

Removing a cigar from between his teeth, Randall

leaned back and answered, "I'm here to gamble, see the sights, and die."

Die was the one word Levi could agree on.

"Die? You're too ornery and no good to die. You'll live another hundred years. You know ole Saint Peter doesn't want you," Clark howled.

"You're right, and my other issue is the devil doesn't want me either, so where does a man like me go once I'm dead?" Randall asked, laughing.

Everyone around the table also broke out in laughter, except Levi, who stood glaring at Randall.

Noticing Levi's hard stare, Randall asked, "You look serious, Sheriff. Come sit down. Let's play a hand or two, unless you're not a gambler."

"I don't play cards or partake in any gambling," Levi said.

"Smart man," Randall said.

"Smart only because he'd lose a month's wages against you, Randall," Clark blared.

The small crowd again burst into laughter.

"You're staying a while in town, then?" Levi asked.

Giving him a quick glance out of the corner of his eye, Randall replied with a question.. "Is there something wrong, Sheriff?"

"I'm just wondering what a gambler and cutthroat like yourself is doing in my town," Levi said.

Everyone grew silent.

Randall put his cards down, removed his cigar again, and gave Levi a quizzical stare. "Have I wronged you, Sheriff?"

Clark put his arm around Levi's shoulders and said, "Come now, son, this isn't your town, it's mine."

"I want to know what he's doing here," Levi said again.

"Sheriff Bass, what in tarnation is wrong with you?" Clark asked.

"Marshal, I'm just trying to get a straight answer from a crooked man, that's all," Levi replied.

"Sheriff, I'm asking again, have I done you wrong? If I have, please tell me so we can sort this out," Randall said.

"Do you want me to be honest?" Levi asked, his hand slowly moving towards the back strap of his Colt.

"Please do, Sheriff, tell me," Randall said.

"Levi Bass, what are you doing here?" Katherine shouted from the lobby of the hotel.

Hearing his wife's voice, Levi spun around and asked, "Katherine, what are you doing here?"

Behind Katherine, Thompson came in. When he saw Levi, he mouthed, "I'm sorry."

Katherine raced over to Levi, stopping a foot away, placed her hands on her hips, and exclaimed, "You had me worried sick. You were supposed to be home for dinner."

"But—" Levi protested.

"Best you get on home, Sheriff, before the ole wife puts you in handcuffs." Clark laughed.

The once tense crowd erupted into hysterics.

Grabbing Levi by the arm, Katherine pulled with all her might, but he didn't budge.

"Katherine, please go outside," Levi whispered into her ear.

She leaned in close and replied, "That's not going to happen. Now it's time you come home before something awful happens here."

"But—" he again protested.

"I won't hear any more until we get back to the house," she said and again tugged on his arm. This time he relented.

"Good night, Sheriff, maybe we'll get to catch up later," Randall joked.

Levi craned his head back and sneered.

Katherine pulled him outside and shoved him with all her might. "What are you thinking? Huh? Were you going to just shoot him down?"

"It's him, Katherine; he's the one responsible," Levi countered.

"No one is responsible for what happened to your family but your father, and you forgave him years ago. No one made your father go to the saloon that night, no one made him gamble, and no one put that gun in his hand. He did it all by himself!" she said, her tone scolding.

"That scoundrel in there taunted him that night. My father was this close to walking away. I was there, I begged that man not to play him, but he did, and then he taunted him. He drove my father to gamble that night and ultimately set him on the course to kill my mother!" Levi shouted.

Several passersby gave Levi and Katherine looks as they walked by.

"Come, we'll continue this conversation at home in private," Katherine said.

He pulled his arm away from her and said, "No, I swore I'd deal with him if I ever saw him, and now he's here, he's right in there."

She stepped up to Levi; only an inch separated them. "If you go in there and shoot him down in front of those people, you'll be arrested and hanged for murder."

"No, I'll—"

"Stop, no, you won't weave a story that will be believable to a court. You'll be arrested, tried and convicted for the murder, then hanged in the gallows outside the city jail. I won't let you throw your life and your family's away like your father did."

"Don't say that," he spat.

Taking his face in her hands, she slowed the tempo of her speech and softly said, "My dear, sweet husband. You've carried the scars of what happened that night for years. I've been by your side and we dealt with them. You found it in your heart to forgive your father. You think by killing that man, you'll complete the circle of violence, but you won't, it will only extend it further. How will your son deal with your hanging? How will we survive? What will happen to us? I know you know this; you have one more person to forgive for that night."

"I won't forgive him, never," Levi said.

"That man did nothing that night, and I'm not talking about forgiving him. I'm telling you to forgive yourself," Katherine said.

Her words hit him like a bullet to the heart.

"You know what I'm saying is true," she said.

"I love you with every fiber in my being, and tonight

I'll walk away, but I can't guarantee what will happen if I see him again. There's a fire that rages in me, and I think the only way to quench it is by killing him," he confessed.

"Come, let's go. Zeke is waiting for you. He's excited to hear about the news today," Katherine said, spoiling the fact that she already knew about the letter.

"How do you know? Did Thompson tell you?"

"No, the postman told me when he delivered our mail," she confessed.

"I was so happy. I was on my way to tell you when Deputy Thompson came into the office and divulged that Pritchard was in town. I haven't been the same since," Levi said.

"Please come home with me. Let's go celebrate what will be our new life soon. We will put this behind us, okay?" Katherine asked.

"Okay."

"You're a good man, Levi Bass," she said.

"No, I'm not. I have hate in my heart," he replied.

"I said good, not perfect. We're human; we sin. I think you should go to confession tomorrow with Father McKenna."

"Good idea," he said.

Nudging for him to go, she said, "Now, please let's go home."

He looked back at the hotel. A roar of cackling echoed onto the street from inside. The urge to race in and do what he'd imagined doing all his life tugged at him, but he now had other obligations more important than an old grudge. He gave in to her but was truthful when he told her he wasn't sure if he could contain his rage.

CHAPTER FOUR

JUNE 13, 1896

PHOENIX, ARIZONA TERRITORY

Levi stared at the church. He'd promised Katherine he'd go, but he couldn't find it in him. He knew she'd ask the moment he came home that night, but he'd just have to deal with her disappointment and try another day.

Much of the shock from yesterday had worn off. The desire to go find Randall and murder him had subsided, and for that he was thankful. What he needed to do was just avoid the man at all costs. He practiced that by taking a long way to his office, which had him bypassing the street in front of the hotel.

He entered his office to find Thompson springing to his feet upon seeing him.

"Sheriff, first let me say how sorry I am. I tried not to say a word, but Mrs. Bass has a way of persuasion. Please, I beg you to forgive me," Thompson groveled.

Levi removed his hat and headed straight for his desk.

"Sheriff, please don't fire me," Thompson begged.

"Deputy Thompson, I'm not going to fire you, but I am reluctant to trust you going forward," Levi said then continued. "In retrospect, I want to thank you for telling her. If she hadn't come, something terrible would have happened."

"Were you going to kill him?" Thompson asked, intrigued by the mystery of Levi's anger towards Randall.

"Randall Pritchard is a low-down dog. He might have become famous for some of his exploits, but he's nothing more than scum. He's swindled and killed for pennies."

"You really don't like him. Did you lose at poker to him?" Thompson asked.

"No, but someone I know did, and it didn't end well," Levi replied.

"Who?"

"No one you know, and it doesn't matter. Soon I'll be gone and you'll be acting sheriff. Now what we should be working on is hiring another deputy so you'll have someone to help you," Levi said.

"C'mon, Sheriff, who did Pritchard beat that you know?" Thompson asked.

"I'm not having this conversation anymore. Have you got someone in mind to hire?" Levi asked, desperately wanting to move the topic to something else.

Ignoring Levi, Thompson continued, but now it was about last night. "You were the talk of the dining hall last night. Everyone was asking why you had it in for Pritchard. There's much speculation around town."

"What do I have to say so we'll stop talking about this?" Levi asked, falling into his chair and leaning back, his arms wrapped around the back of his head.

"Who was it that Pritchard played?"

"I'm not saying. Now, damn it, Thompson, you were worried I'd fire you, and now I think I might just to get you to shut up!" Levi blared.

Thompson lowered his gaze and sheepishly replied, "Sorry, Sheriff."

The office door burst open and in came Clark.

"Not now!" Levi exclaimed.

"Sheriff Bass!" Clark howled, slamming the door behind him.

"I'm not talking about last night," Levi shot back.

Clark pulled a chair from the far wall and placed it in front of Levi's desk. "I'm not letting you off that easy. What got into you last night?"

"Marshal, I don't want to talk about Randall Pritchard or what happened last night," Levi said, desperately not wanting to discuss the situation with Randall.

"No, you have some explaining to do. Randall is well known, and his being in Phoenix will bring travelers to come to see him," Clark said.

Leaning onto his desk, Levi asked, "You want more gamblers and cutthroats to come to town? His being here will only breed a culture we don't want here in Phoenix or the county at large."

"What happened between you and him? Clearly there's a past that only you know, 'cause I asked him if he knows you, and he doesn't," Clark said.

As Clark and Levi went back and forth, Thompson went back to his desk and sat down. He was riveted by the conversation.

"Marshal, I don't have a past with Mr. Pritchard. I just know his reputation and don't want him in my county," Levi lied.

"I'll remind you again, this is my town. How about I worry if Randall is good for this town or not, and you concern yourself outside the town limits," Clark said, his tone turning angry.

Levi looked at the clock on the wall and said, "Marshal, thank you for coming, Deputy Thompson and I need to get to work."

Clark stood and said, "Sheriff, please don't show up and threaten Mr. Pritchard again. If you do, I'll arrest you for disturbing the peace."

Levi clenched his jaw tight and withheld saying anything.

Clark spun around and left the office, slamming the door hard.

Levi shot a look to Thompson and said, "No more about Pritchard."

"Yes, Sheriff."

"Let's get to work, and again, no more talk," Levi warned.

***

Randall wiped his mouth and tossed the napkin on the table. He had scheduled to have breakfast with Jane, but she hadn't shown. Not one to pry into anyone's business, he decided against going to her room to check on her.

As he left the dining hall, Dale called out, "Mr. Pritchard, I have something for you."

Randall approached the counter and asked, "Is it the information I was seeking about Savannah Stone?"

"Yes, sir, it is," Dale said, handing him an envelope. "A man dropped it off not long ago."

Randall took it, left a small tip, and walked off. He ripped the envelope open to find a single piece of paper; on it was detailed where Savannah lived and her current marital status, which was marked as widow. He hadn't heard about her husband's demise, so it must have been recent.

Over the years he had kept track of her by the use of hired investigators. It was the only way for him to know how she was doing, since she never wrote him back and had in so many words told him one time that she wanted nothing to do with him. It pained him not to have a relationship with his only child, but it was what it was, and he would again try to mend the fences that were long ago shorn.

"Where are you off to?" Jane said from the stairwell.

Randall spun around to see her descending slowly. Her grip along the bannister was firm as if she was carefully watching her step. He met her at the bottom and offered his hand. "Good morning."

She allowed him to kiss her hand and blushed like a teenaged girl. "Well, good morning. I do have to apologize for being late for our scheduled breakfast. I overslept. I had the worst coughing fit last night and didn't sleep well."

Randall glanced into the dining hall and saw ample tables available. "How about we go grab a table?"

"Heavens no, you go about your day; I'm just sorry I missed our breakfast," she said.

He slid the envelope into his coat pocket, lifted his arm, and said, "Let's go eat."

She took his arm and the two sauntered into the dining hall.

They both ordered eggs, firm, with a side of bacon and toast.

"I'm sorry to hear you had a tough night," Randall said.

"Thank you, but I'm used to it now. I just feel horrible for the maid. I left one of the towels covered in blood," she said, her hands folded tightly on top of the table.

Hearing how bad her consumption was made him feel horrible for her. He reached across the table and took her hand. "I hope I'm not being too forward."

She looked at his rough and wrinkled hand and smiled. "No, it's perfect. I've forgotten how good it feels to have human contact."

"Me too," he said. "And going forward if you need me, if I can help with anything, please let me know."

"I don't want to trouble you. Let's just enjoy our company," she said.

"Like you said yesterday, we were meant to meet, we have a connection, I know that is a fact. We're in this mortal death spiral together, so please call on me for anything," he said.

"I will agree to that if you reciprocate," she said, looking longingly into his eyes.

He paused to think about what he was about to say and decided to just let go. "I agree."

"It appeared you struggled with that," she said.

"I did. It's not in my nature," he replied.

"I'm going to make that a goal," she said.

"Goal?"

"I'm going to change that about your nature," she said sweetly.

"You are, are ya?" he asked, chuckling.

"I think you'll find out that I'm a determined person. When I set my mind to something, it tends to happen," she countered.

"What are you doing for dinner?" he asked.

"How about we go somewhere and picnic?" she asked.

"I would love to, but I can't. I have some business to attend to today," he said as his mind went to Savannah.

"Another day, then," she said.

Wanting to be open and honest and thinking she could provide valuable counsel on how to deal with his daughter, he said, "I'm going to check on my daughter."

Her eyes widened. "You have a daughter in Phoenix?"

"I do."

"Oh, how wonderful for you to have that support," she said.

"Thing is, she doesn't know I'm here, and if she did, she probably wouldn't want to see me," he confessed.

"You're estranged?"

"That's a nice way of putting it." He laughed. After a good chuckle, he stopped and said, "Since we're being open and honest, I should tell you everything about me."

Sincerely curious, she leaned back in her chair and waited for him to begin.

"I'm a well-known gambler and some would say gunslinger," Randall said then paused to wait for her response.

However, Jane sat emotionless.

Seeing she wasn't going to respond, he continued, "Let it be known the gunslinger moniker comes from having to defend myself. I've never killed someone premeditatedly or did so out of anger. I was always defending myself."

Still Jane sat not saying a word or emoting.

"My former wife didn't approve of what I did even though she knew what I did before we wed. She was fine with it then and with the monies I garnered and the lifestyle she became accustomed to. After Savannah was born, she changed her mind suddenly. We spent the first three years of Savannah's life arguing about my gambling, with her insisting I give it up. I refused, and one night I returned home to find she'd left with Savannah and with most of my winnings I had stashed. She left me a note telling me not to find her and Savannah. I'd be lying if I said I wasn't relieved. Those three years were miserable, she made my life very difficult, but I missed Savannah. I then thought that maybe she was right and the life of a gambler and that of a family man weren't compatible. I relented to her wishes and never visited although I kept tabs on them and have since followed Savannah's life. She and her now deceased husband relocated here not long ago from Tucson."

"And you haven't seen her yet?' Jane asked, breaking her silence.

"No," he answered.

"Were you planning on doing that today?" she asked.

He looked away and thought about what he'd say.

"You're not sure how to approach her?" she said, probing.

He shot her a look and said, "Correct."

"Can I give some advice here?" she asked.

"I'd love some. Relationships haven't been my strong suit, specifically the father-daughter kind," he said.

"I believe in being honest, and lead from love."

"It's that simple?"

"I'm suggesting you do that, but any way you try may not be successful. Have you ever tried to reach out over the years?" Jane asked.

"After her mother died, I did, and she promptly wrote me back and told me to stay out of her life," he answered.

"Did you ever try again?"

"Yes, and I got the same response; then I stopped getting replies at all. I then began to hire investigators to keep tabs on her. I traced her to Tucson then to here," Randall said.

"If you stopped by her house, you think she'd tell you to leave?" Jane asked.

"I guarantee she would," he replied.

"So what were you planning on doing today?"

"I was going to, and I know this sounds horrible, spy on her. Follow her around, see where she goes, what she does; try to get an idea of what her day is like, then make an attempt to go see her," Randall said.

"Normally I would say spying on someone was odd, but in this situation I would agree. It will help you get a full picture of who she is, but she might spot you," Jane said.

"I don't think she knows what I look like, or at least I doubt she does," Randall said.

"Then go check on her; see what her day is like. In the meantime I'll think of a way you can approach her," Jane said.

"Is saying checking on her a more polite way of saying spying?" Randall laughed.

"Yes, it is," she said just as she caught the eye of the waiter coming their way. "Looks like our food is coming."

"Good, I'm starving."

She reached out and touched his hand. "It will work out, just believe it."

"I've never told anyone about my daughter."

"Thank you for trusting in me," she said.

The waiter returned and set their plates down. "Can I get you anything else?"

They both replied no.

He rushed off.

"Shall we dig in?" Randall asked.

"Yes, let's do," Jane answered.

When they were finished, she looked up at him and said, "I have to thank you for doing this. I know you must be stuffed after eating two meals."

"Now why would you say that?" he asked.

"On account when I saw you this morning, I saw that on the top of your shirt," she said, pointing to a spot of jelly.

He looked down but still couldn't see it. "Where?"

She got up and walked over to him. She took her napkin, wetted the tip in a glass of water, and wiped away the evidence from his first breakfast. "There, all better."

Unable to control the urge to kiss her, he brought her close, their noses almost touching, and said, "Thank you."

Her breathing slowed and she purred, "You're welcome."

He covered the remaining distance and gingerly kissed her lips.

She received his kiss and returned one of her own. A smile stretched across her face when she pulled back. "That was nice."

"It was," he said, smiling, a warmth running through his body.

The waiter approached and cleared his throat. "Excuse me, is that all this morning?"

Jane recoiled and went to her seat.

Annoyed by the waiter's dreadful timing, Randall growled, "Nothing more, and go away."

The waiter rushed off.

"People are so rude these days. Where have their manners gone, these darn youngsters," Randall complained.

"It's fine," she said.

He looked at his pocket watch and said, "I should be

starting my day."

"You mean checking on Savannah?"

"Yes," he said, pushing away from the table. He stood and stepped next to her chair. He offered his arm and she took it.

The two walked to the lobby.

Stopping near the entrance, Jane asked, "How do you know what she looks like if you haven't seen her since she was three years old?"

"I don't know what she looks like. I know where she lives; that will be where I start," he replied.

She squeezed his arm and said, "I wish you luck today."

"What will you be doing with your fine day?" he asked.

"I'll keep busy by doing a bit of crochet, and I think I'll write some letters," she answered.

He leaned in and gave her a peck on the cheek. "Have a good day. I'll see you for dinner."

She blushed and said, "Yes, dinner sounds wonderful."

He donned the top of his head with his wide-brimmed hat, gave her a toothy grin, and exited the hotel.

***

Randall went to Savannah's house just as she was leaving. Assuming it was her, he followed her all the way back to town, ensuring he kept his distance so as not to elicit suspicion.

Savannah rode up to Montgomery's General Store,

applied the brake, and jumped down. She took a deep breath and walked into the establishment.

Randall hitched his horse across the street and hurried across and into the store. There he found Savannah talking to a man behind a counter.

"I saw the sign in the window yesterday about employment. I'd like to apply for the position," she said, standing tall to the man, whose name was Barry Montgomery and who also happened to be the owner.

"You want to work here stocking shelves and loading customers' wagons?" he asked her with a puzzled look on his face.

"Mr. Montgomery, you know me and know my husband has recently passed. I'm in a tight pinch with the bank and need the money. I'm a very hard worker. I'm strong and could really help you out. I think I should also tell you that I'm very trustworthy and good with keeping books should you need me to help with that," she said confidently.

"You're good with numbers? Did you go to school?" he asked.

"I did; I went through eighth grade. My mother saw the importance of education," she said.

"Hmm, can I think about it?" he asked, showing reluctance at the proposition.

"Mr. Montgomery, I've seen that sign up there for over a week; that tells me you're having trouble filling the position. I'm here now, able-bodied and can help; I can start immediately," she said.

Rubbing his chin as he thought, he said, "I just don't

know, Mrs. Stone."

Overhearing all of this, Randall felt for his daughter. He wanted to approach her and say that all would be fine, but knew the timing would only backfire.

"Please, Mr. Montgomery, you'd be doing me a favor," Savannah pleaded.

"I'll tell you what, come back tomorrow and I'll have an answer," he said.

She sighed and said, "Very well, I'll be back this time tomorrow." She turned and walked out.

Randall watched her leave then approached Montgomery. "My name is Randall Pritchard."

"Yes, sir, I know who you are; you've been in a couple of times, gotten the newspaper. You're that gambler they've been talking about."

"I am."

"How can I help you?" Montgomery asked.

"I overheard your conversation with that young woman. I want you to hire her immediately," Randall said.

"Excuse me," Montgomery said.

"I want you to hire her and pay her a substantial wage, one that she deserves," Randall ordered.

"Sir, with all due respect, this is my establishment, and I hire who I see fit, and having a woman in here isn't going to work for what I need," Montgomery replied.

"Listen, Mr. Montgomery, I do understand that you need to hire someone adequate, and you can. I want you to hire her, and I'll pay her wages," Randall said, pulling out his wallet. He removed a few hundred-dollar bills and set them on the counter.

Wide eyed, Montgomery looked at the money then at Randall. "I don't understand."

"You're going to help me help that woman," Randall said.

"Why don't you give her the money?" Montgomery asked.

"On account I know she won't take it. She doesn't like charity, like she said. She's a hard worker, a woman with impeccable integrity. Now go tell her you've made your decision," Randall said.

Scooping the bills off the counter, Montgomery said, "Yes, sir." He rushed out of the store to find Savannah climbing up onto the wagon. "Mrs. Stone, hold up there."

Savannah shot him a look and said, "If it's bad news, I don't want to hear it. I've heard enough lately."

"On the contrary, Mrs. Stone, I've considered your employment and have come to a decision."

"You're going to hire me?" she asked gleefully.

"Yes, I am, but I'll have you work my books and do errands around the counter. I'll also be taking on a hand to help with deliveries and such," Montgomery said, finding his situation better off with two people hired but only having to pay one.

Savannah jumped from the wagon and ran up to him. She restrained herself from hugging him and instead offered her hand.

Montgomery took it and shook. "You can start—"

"I'll go to work now," she exclaimed.

"Do you want to know your wage?" Montgomery asked.

Randall stepped out of the store and stood watching the interaction.

Catching that Randall was there, Montgomery answered Savannah, "I'll pay you ten dollars per week."

"Ten dollars per week? Mr. Montgomery, that's a lot," she said.

"Well, Mrs. Stone, I know you need the help, so it seems fair," he replied.

Randall smiled.

"I want to give you a big hug and kiss," Savannah chirped.

"Now if you want to go inside, I'll go over some details about how I run the store," Montgomery said.

Savannah hopped onto the walkway and strutted past Randall and back into the store.

Montgomery walked up and asked, "Is ten enough per week?"

"Sure, but I expect you'll give her bonuses too," Randall said. "And, Mr. Montgomery, don't take advantage of your position over her."

"I don't know what you mean," Montgomery said.

"You're a man, she's a young woman, don't get confused, so keep it professional," Randall warned.

"I understand, and I'll have you know I'm married and don't do such things," Montgomery blared.

"Don't take offense. I always make sure people I do business with understand the terms of the arrangement so there's no misunderstandings," Randall said. "And one last thing, she's not to know I did this."

"She won't know a thing," Montgomery replied.

"Good, now have a good day," Randall said and walked off with a feeling of accomplishment surging through him.

LA JUNTA, COLORADO

The train came to a jerky stop outside the depot. Fester lifted his hat off his weary face and peered out the window. "Where are we?" he asked out loud, hoping someone would answer.

An elderly woman he'd had a conversation with along the ride from Dodge City replied, "La Junta, Colorado. It's a scheduled stop."

"Good," Fester said, rising to his feet and scooting out into the aisle. "How long before we leave?" he asked a conductor just a few feet away, who was busy helping other passengers.

"One hour, sir, if you're continuing on to Santa Fe, New Mexico Territory," the conductor said as he grabbed a piece of luggage for a young woman who was disembarking.

Fester exited the train, stretched and inhaled deeply. He would enjoy the hour stop and hoped the telegram he'd sent late yesterday had been received.

"Is that you, Silvester!" a voice boomed in the distance.

Fester craned his head and looked around for the source, but the sea of people coming and going made it difficult.

"Over here, Silvester!" the voice cried out.

Fester continued to look but didn't see anyone. A hand gripped his shoulder and spun him around. "Cousin Theodore?"

The two men embraced.

Fester pulled back from the embrace and looked at his younger cousin. He was tall, lean and looked very capable. Strapped to his back was a thick leather satchel, and around his waist he wore a gun belt, a Colt Single Action Army in the holster. "I see you got my telegram."

"I did, and I don't go by Theodore, just call me Ted."

"How about I call you retribution?" Fester said.

"I'm so sorry about Ronald; I liked him a lot. I know it's been a while since we've seen each other, but I considered him like a brother," Ted said.

"It's a tragedy. He was gunned down like a common dog. I left Michigan the second I got word and made my way to Dodge City. I put his body on the train back to Lansing early this morning."

"May he rest in peace," Ted said, lowering his head slightly.

"You've grown tall and sturdy, cousin," Fester said, patting Ted on the shoulder. "How old are you now?"

"Almost eighteen, and my pa says it's this good Colorado air and hard work that makes one strong," Ted said.

"Speaking of your pa, what did he say about you leaving?" Fester asked.

"He and ma talked a lot about the telegram, but he said it wasn't our fight and told me not to come join you. He's a coward, so I snuck off the farm this afternoon," Ted replied.

"Thank you," Fester said.

"We're going to serve some righteous justice to that old coot," Ted howled with youthful confidence. "Is anyone else going to join us?"

"I sent word to our cousin in New Mexico Territory too," Fester replied. "Are you sure you're good with doing this?"

"I wouldn't want to be doing anything else," Ted said. A broad smile creased across his smooth and chiseled face.

"Are you good with that?" Fester asked, motioning to his pistol. "The man we're going up against is a known gunslinger. He's killed many men."

"Am I good? Hell yes!" Ted said, tearing the Colt from his holster and twirling it on his finger before holstering it again. "I practice daily."

"Do you model yourself after Wyatt Earp or something?" Fester joked.

"How soon before we go?" Ted asked.

"An hour," Fester answered.

Ted threw his arm over Fester's shoulder and said, "Let's go get ourselves a drink, catch up, and talk about how we're going to get payback for your brother."

"I like the sound of that," Fester said.

The two marched off to a small bar located near the far side of the depot.

CHAPTER FIVE

JUNE 14, 1896

OUTSKIRTS OF PHOENIX, MARICOPA COUNTY, ARIZONA TERRITORY

L evi leaned over the edge of the rock outcropping and looked down on the man whose body was hanging by the neck, the rope secured to a large boulder next to Thompson. He removed his hat, wiped his sweaty brow with his sleeve, and asked, "Do you suppose he killed himself, or did someone do this?"

"Hard to know, Sheriff," Thompson replied, looking down at the body as it swayed in the gentle breeze.

Levi and Thompson had only found out about the body an hour before when two laborers from a nearby ranch came to the sheriff's office and notified them that they'd found the body earlier that morning. Upon receiving the news, both Levi and Thompson rode out. It wasn't every day they encountered a dead body, especially one hanging over a ravine.

"I suppose we should cut him down and see if we can

find out who it is," Levi said, pulling out his sheath knife. He knelt down and cut the rope that was tied around a boulder. He slid the blade over the rope twice before it snapped and sent the body falling the remaining twenty feet to the bottom of the ravine below, landing with a thud.

"Saddle up. Let's go get 'im," Levi said.

The two slowly made their way to the bottom.

After a quick examination of the body, they discovered several bullet holes, one in the man's shoulder, one in his leg, and one through his right hand. By the condition of the man's forearms, it was apparent he'd been in a fight.

"This man was murdered," Levi said.

"It certainly looks that way, Sheriff," Thompson said.

Rolling the man over onto his back, he looked carefully at his bloated face and asked, "Do you recognize him?"

"Ah, no."

"Me either," Levi said.

"Oh wait, can you turn his head?" Thompson asked.

Levi did as he was asked.

"Right there, that mark, it's a scar. That's Charlie Torrance. He works for Mr. Deveron."

"Mr. Deveron the orange grove owner in Scottsdale?" Levi asked.

"That's the one. Is there another Mr. Deveron?"

"Not that I'm aware of. Let's load him on your horse. Take him to the undertaker, and after that go back to the office," Levi said.

"Will you not be coming with me, Sheriff?"

Thompson asked.

Standing up, Levi looked north and said, "No, I won't be. I'm heading to see Mr. Deveron and see what I can find out about Charlie Torrance and why the poor son of a bitch was left dangling out here."

PHOENIX, ARIZONA TERRITORY

Savannah showed up to the store five minutes early. She attempted to enter but found the door locked. Waiting outside, she watched with joy as people casually walked by. She couldn't believe her good fortune in getting a job so quickly and was filled with hope that she'd be able to keep the house and land.

The lock on the door clacked loudly.

She turned to see Mr. Montgomery standing there.

He opened the door fully and said with a slight yawn, "Good morning, Mrs. Stone."

Hopping to her feet with bountiful joy, she said, "Good morning, Mr. Montgomery." She rushed to the door, stopping only because he was in her way.

"You're very eager this morning, aren't you?" he asked, not expecting to see her so excited.

"I told you I was a hard worker," she said.

"Then come on in and start where you finished yesterday," Montgomery said, stepping out of her way.

Savannah marched in and towards the back office.

Just as he was closing the door, Randall appeared.

"Mr. Prit—"

Before he could say his name, Randall cut him off.

"Don't mention my name around here, not in front of her."

Montgomery nodded.

"Step outside for a minute," Randall said.

Doing as he said, Montgomery closed the door. "What can I do for ya?"

"How's it going?"

"Well, very well, she seems like she's smart and took to balancing my books with ease. She also seems to have a knack for inventory. I'm impressed since she's a woman," Montgomery said, exposing his sexism.

"I knew she'd do well," Randall said.

"Who is she to you anyway?"

"Just someone who needs help, and I like to give it…anonymously."

"It will stay that way, I promise you that," Montgomery said.

"Good, now if you'll step out of my way, I'd like to go inside," Randall said.

Montgomery opened the door for him. "Will you be needing the paper?"

Crossing the threshold, Randall replied, "Yes, I will."

Savannah looked towards the door when she heard it open. "Good morning, sir. What can I help you with?" she asked Randall, unaware he was her father.

"A newspaper and some other items," Randall replied nervously.

Savannah stopped what she was doing and grabbed a newspaper. She placed it on the counter.

"A pound of licorice and a box of cigars, the

Dominicans, also," Randall said, walking up to the counter.

Savannah opened the licorice jar and, using a set of tongs, pulled out some and placed them on the scale. Adjusting the amount to equal a pound, she picked them up and placed them on a piece of brown paper and folded it up. She turned around, found the cigars, and asked, "A box of thirty or the fifty count?"

"Fifty, I'm a big smoker," Randall said.

She took the box and set it in front of him. With a broad smile stretched across her face, she asked, "Anything else, sir."

"You're new here," he said.

"Just started yesterday, as a matter of fact. Mr. Montgomery was thoughtful enough to bring me on."

"That's very nice of him," Randall said just as he gave Montgomery a quick glance.

"It was very nice of him, considering my situation," she said.

"Situation?"

"It's personal, but I needed the job," she answered.

"I can only assume it's financial. Sorry to hear that," Randall said.

"Money, I hate it, but until they find something else that pays for everything, I'll just have to keep working."

"I see you're married. Is your husband not working?"

Wanting to ignore the question, she asked, "Will there be anything else?"

Randall looked past her to the shelves to see if he could find something else. "Oh, let's see, how about some perfume, do you have any?"

"We do," Savannah answered, turning around to a small cabinet. She removed two bottles and set them on the counter. "I'll have to admit that I haven't smelled their scent."

Randall picked up one of the bottles and examined it. He was about as far away from understanding such things as he could be. He pinched the sprayer bulb; a spritz of aromatic shot out, hitting him in the face. He recoiled, set the bottle down, and howled.

Savannah giggled like a schoolgirl at Randall.

Watching the episode from afar, Montgomery marched over and snapped, "Don't laugh at the customer."

"I'm sorry, sir," Savannah said, her demeanor turning serious.

Randall wiped his face, shot Montgomery a harsh look, and said, "Don't get on the girl. It was funny. I looked like a damn fool, and she was right to laugh."

"We pride ourselves on respecting our customers here," Montgomery said.

"I apologize, sir," Savannah said.

"You were fine," Randall said softly. "Now that I've not only smelled but tasted this fine perfume, I think I'll buy it."

"You will?" Savannah asked.

"I will. Wrap it up in a box, if you could, for me, a pretty box, and put a bow on it," Randall said, thinking he wanted to give this to Jane at dinner.

Savannah hurried away with the perfume to wrap.

"Can I help you with anything else?" Montgomery asked.

"I'll wait for the girl to come back," Randall replied.

Savannah returned promptly, the perfume packaged to Randall's specifications. "Here you go, sir. Can I help you with anything else?"

"I can't think of anything, no, but if I need something else, I'll be sure to return," Randall said.

"Very well," Savannah replied. She picked up a pencil and jotted some numbers on a notepad. "Everything comes to eleven dollars and thirteen cents." She found a brown sack and set all the items inside, carefully folded the top, and slid it across the counter to him.

Randall removed his wallet, handed her a twenty-dollar bill, and said, "Thank you for your help today, and please keep the change."

Holding the bill in her hands, she gave Randall a surprised look. "Are you sure, sir? That is a lot of money."

"I'm quite positive. You've been very helpful," Randall said with a smile, picking up the sack that contained his items. He tipped his hat to her and continued, "You have a wonderful day, little lady; I'll be seeing you soon."

"You too, sir, have a blessed day," she said, a large smiled gracing her tender face. Her eyes were twinkling with excitement at the large tip she'd just received.

Elation swept over Randall as he departed the store. She was more than he ever imagined. From the lovable three-year-old he'd left years ago, she'd turned into a beautiful, sweet, smart, strong and vibrant woman. He was happy that she'd turned into someone a father could be proud of. He only wished he could now turn back the clock and see her grow, he thought as he walked towards the hotel with his sack of goods tucked under his arm. Then he remembered the man he had been at that time. Would she have grown to be like she was with him as an influence? It was hard to know and foolish to even contemplate. He could never get back those years, they were lost to time; but he did have these moments, and he would cherish them. What he needed to figure out soon was how to share with her that he wasn't the villain her mother had painted him out to be, so they could spend what remaining days he had together.

SCOTTSDALE, ARIZONA TERRITORY

Mr. Deveron was a tall, slender man with short-cropped gray hair and a thick white beard. He'd moved to Arizona from California on the heels of Winfield Scott's arrival. Upon laying his eyes on the terrain, he came to the same conclusion that Scott had: this land could be used for agriculture if they could irrigate it properly, and so he did. Oranges were already being grown there, so he didn't fool around with other crops and went with what was working, oranges.

He had acquired three hundred and sixty-seven acres at four dollars an acre and went to work planting trees. He knew it would take years before his trees would start to produce, but that didn't deter him.

Having such an expansive grove, he needed men to work it, and Charlie Torrance was one of them.

"Are you sure it was Charlie?" Deveron asked as he

paced his office.

"My deputy confirmed his identity from a scar on his neck," Levi replied.

"Was it shaped like a crescent moon?" Deveron asked, pointing to his own neck and making the shape of the scar.

"Yes, it was," Levi said. "With the other wounds on the body, we know for sure he was murdered. What I'm trying to determine is who did it. What can you tell me about the men Charlie ran with or knew?"

Deveron let out a heavy sigh and said, "I liked that boy. He was a real hard worker. He started working for me a month after I arrived from Ventura and was very reliable. Never missed a day of work until this week when he didn't show up two days ago."

"So he didn't come to work two days ago?"

"Correct."

"And again, whom did he run with? Did you know of anyone whom he had disagreements with? Did he owe anyone money?" Levi asked.

Taking a seat in a large leather chair, Deveron crossed his legs and mumbled, "Gambling."

"What was that?" Levi asked.

"Oh, that damn boy got himself involved in gambling. Was bragging a few days ago about how he'd won a lot of money from some fellas back in Phoenix," Deveron said.

"Who?"

"Oh, heck, I can't remember. I'm not good with names," Deveron replied.

"These could be the men who killed Charlie. Please think," Levi urged.

"You know who would know? Let's ask Phil. Those two worked together; there's a good chance he'd know," Deveron said, getting to his feet. He left the office but quickly returned. "It's your luck, Sheriff, Phil was just out back."

Walking in just behind Deveron was Phil. He was a small man, standing about five feet six with small features from his hands to his feet. He removed his hat and sheepishly looked at Levi.

"Who was Charlie Torrance gambling with?" Levi asked.

"He said he'd become friends with a fella named Brant Stone who lived in Phoenix," Phil answered.

The name sounded familiar to Levi though he couldn't quite place it. "Anyone else?"

"Yeah, there were some other fellas," Phil replied.

"I need their names," Levi pressed.

"Al and Samuel," Phil said. He scrunched his face as he thought hard to make sure he had the right names. "Yeah, some fellas named Al and Samuel. Last I saw him a few days ago, he said he had a big gambling party to attend at some farmhouse outside Phoenix. He left later that night; haven't seen him since. Is he okay?"

"No, he's not okay. I found Charlie hanging by the neck near Painted Rock north of Phoenix," Levi replied.

Phil did the sign of the cross like a good Catholic, pressed his eyes closed tight, and said, "Oh, dear lord."

"Phil, is there any other information that you feel would help me catch whoever killed Charlie?" Levi asked.

"No, Sheriff. I only know he was gambling a lot in

town and had run into those other fellas a couple of months or so ago along with Brant Stone, who is also dead…oh no, Sheriff, do you suppose those fellas also killed Brant Stone?"

"Brant Stone is dead?" Levi asked, shocked to hear it.

"Yes, Sheriff, he died almost two months ago. Fell off his horse and hit his head against a rock is what I heard," Phil said.

Suddenly Levi recalled where he'd heard the name Brant Stone before.

Seeing Levi was lost in thought, Phil asked, "Anything else, Sheriff?"

"No, you've been very helpful," Levi said. He turned to Deveron. "Thank you for being cooperative."

"If I can do anything else to help find those brutal murderers, don't hesitate to call on me," Deveron said.

Levi shook both men's hands and promptly left. He had been given valuable information that he felt could lead him to the killers, and quite possibly to another murder.

PHOENIX, ARIZONA TERRITORY

Upon opening the box, Jane's eyes widen with joy. "Randall Pritchard, you're too generous," she said, removing the bottle of perfume and admiring its shape and the purple tassel that dangled from the spray pump.

"Now be careful. Don't press that thingy right there and have it pointed towards your face," Randall said, pointing to the sprayer.

"I'm quite familiar with how to use these bottles, and

something tells me you must have sprayed yourself," Jane said.

"I did; don't I smell nice?" Randall joked.

She pointed the nozzle at her chest and squeezed the spray pump once. A mist covered her chest and neck. "Oh, it smells delicious."

"It does," Randall said.

She rose from her seat, walked over to him, and gave him a kiss on the lips. "Thank you."

"You're so welcome," Randall said, wrapping one arm around her waist. "Shall we go into the dining room now or just get ourselves a drink first in the lobby?"

"A drink sounds wonderful," she said, going back to the chair next to him.

Randall motioned to a waiter and ordered two drinks for them. He put his attention back on her, but before he could say anything, she asked, "How did it go today?"

His eyes lit up. "You should have seen her. She's so smart and confident. She's taken to work very well and has even surprised the shop owner with her abilities."

"So the apple didn't fall far from the tree?" Jane quipped.

Randall laughed.

"Go ahead, tell me what happened?" Jane pressed.

"Oh, not much to tell. As you know, I secured her a job at the general store. I went in today, and she assisted me in getting all the things I requested. She was very professional and tended to all my needs."

"She sounds wonderful," Jane said with a pleasant smile.

"She is," Randall said, looking on fondly, thinking of Savannah.

"When do you plan on telling her who you are?" Jane asked.

"Not sure, I'm enjoying the moments now; I'd hate to disrupt them…"

Reaching over and touching his hand, she said, "I'm sure you'll find the right time."

"I wish I had your wisdom about such things. Maybe I should get you to talk for me," he said, thinking about the idea.

"I wouldn't think of encroaching on your personal business," she said.

"You'd do better than me, that's all I know," he said.

She relaxed into her chair and thought about how she would approach Savannah if given the responsibility.

The waiter returned with their drinks and set them on the table in between them. He turned and swiftly walked away.

Randall took his drink in his hand and held it high. "Here's to you."

Taking her glass, she also raised it and said, "No, to you, and to you and your wonderful daughter reuniting."

"Here's to that," he said and touched his glass against hers.

***

Levi knocked on the door.

"Who is it?" Savannah cried out.

"It's Sheriff Bass," Levi replied.

Hearing who it was, Savannah dropped what she was doing and went to the door. She unlocked it and opened it wide. "Evening, Sheriff."

Levi removed his hat and said, "Ma'am, I'm sorry to disturb you at this hour. Are you Mrs. Stone?"

"Does this have to do with the bank?" Savannah blurted out, thinking that somehow Sullivan had already initiated foreclosure proceedings.

"Ah, no, ma'am, I'm here to ask you a few questions concerning your late husband," Levi said.

Savannah hadn't met the sheriff before, but after looking at him, seeing his badge, and going by her intuition, she decided to invite him in. "Sheriff, please come in."

Levi entered the house.

"Please take a seat at the table," Savannah said as she rushed to the small table and pushed items away to clear a spot for him.

Levi took a seat and placed his hat on the table.

"Can I get you something to drink? Some coffee or maybe a cup of water?" Savannah asked.

"No, ma'am, could you please sit so I can ask you a few questions, and then I'll be on my way to leave you to your evening."

Taking a seat at the opposite end of the table, Savannah asked, "How can I help you?"

"Did your husband know a man by the name of Charlie Torrance?" Levi asked.

"Not that I'm aware of."

"What about an Al or Samuel?" Levi asked.

Savannah shook her head and said, "Those names don't sound familiar. Um, Sheriff, what's this to do with?"

"There's been a murder. Happened we think a couple of days ago," Levi replied.

"A murder? How could my husband be involved in a murder a couple of days ago? He's been dead himself for seven weeks."

"I don't think he's involved, but he knew the man murdered. I've received credible information that your husband and the man just found were acquaintances."

"How were they acquaintances?" she asked, growing concerned about where the conversation was going.

"They gambled together, that's what I know," Levi replied.

"Gambled, oh no, my husband wasn't a gambler," she protested.

"Are you sure?"

Savannah paused before she answered and thought about the money that he'd borrowed and the many nights he'd spent away getting drunk. Was that where the money went? Had he lost it all gambling?

"Ma'am, when your husband died, who investigated?" Levi asked although he already knew the answer.

"Marshal Clark did. He said Brant had fallen...wait, do you think Brant was murdered too?" she asked, now connecting the circumstantial evidence.

"I don't know if he was or not, but he was found with a single wound to the head, correct?"

"Yes."

"And he was involved in some sort of gambling with

Charlie Torrance, who is now also dead. I'm not saying he was murdered, but I need to look into this more vigorously."

She lowered her head and placed it into her hands. She could feel a surge of emotion rising in her.

"I'll leave you be, but if you recall anything, please find me at the office in town or have my deputy find me," Levi said then stood.

"He mortgaged the house and land," she mumbled under her breath.

"Excuse me?"

Lifting her head, she looked at Levi. "My husband mortgaged the house and land days before he was found dead. Do you think he lost it gambling?"

"Possibly or he was robbed of it," Levi replied.

She got to her feet and said, "Sheriff, I need you to find out what happened to my husband. If he was a gambler, I need to know, and if he was murdered, those responsible must be brought to justice."

"Mrs. Stone, I can assure you I'll move Heaven and Earth to find out what truly happened to your husband if it was murder."

"Thank you," she said.

"I'll leave you be, Mrs. Stone. Again, I apologize for coming at such an hour with this type of information. Just know that I'm an ally," Levi said. He walked to the door and lifted the latch. "Have a good evening, ma'am."

"Good evening, Sheriff," Savannah said.

Levi exited the house, disappearing into the dark of night.

Savannah closed the door behind him and locked it. Now alone, she allowed the emotions to burst out of her. Tears flowed down her cheeks, and her knees went weak. She toppled to the floor and sobbed. It was apparent now that Brant had lied for weeks about his dealings in Phoenix. He had been gambling but kept it from her because of her father.

Her mind raced with various scenarios that Brant could have been involved with, from extramarital affairs to possibly other children. He was a proven liar, which broke her heart, but she had a feeling she wasn't done with finding out about his other life just yet.

***

Levi spent the ride home thinking about how once more he'd witnessed the collateral damage left by a gambler.

Upon entering his house, he found it dark, his wife having put Zeke to bed and gone to retire in their bedroom. He grabbed something to eat in the kitchen then headed to the bedroom. There he discovered her lying in bed, a single lantern casting a warm orange glow and his wife nestled reading a book.

"How can you read with such poor light?" he asked, closing the door behind him.

"Oh good, you're home. I was growing concerned," she said.

He began to undress. "How was Zeke today?"

"He's well, misses his father, and longs for our move to Prescott," Katherine replied.

"Soon enough," he said.

"I spoke to Father McKenna today," Katherine said, lowering the book and looking at him.

He put on a pair of long underwear and headed for his side of the bed. "I know what you're going to say, and I will go see him, I promise."

"You said you'd go yesterday," she countered.

"Katherine, I have a lot happening, and now I have a murder to investigate before I go," he said, slipping into the bed, the coolness from the sheets permeating the cotton of his undergarments.

"A murder?" she asked.

"Yes, outside town near Painted Rock, a man was hanged and—"

Interrupting him, she said, "I don't need to hear the details."

Patting her hand, he said, "I'll go see Father McKenna when I have time, not before."

"But you promised."

"And I'll keep my word. I just have bigger things to handle at the moment."

"Getting upset and almost shooting a man in cold blood isn't a big thing?" she asked.

"I was too emotional, I've admitted that, and I've done my best to avoid him. I can assure you nothing will happen," he said.

"Just go soon, please," she said, setting her book on the nightstand. She turned down the lantern and slid further down under the sheets and thick down duvet cover.

He did as she did, pulling the sheets up near his chin.

He stared at the ceiling and asked, "Katherine?"

"Yes."

"If I had killed Randall Pritchard, would you still love me?" he asked.

"I'll always love you, always."

"Even if I murdered a man?" he asked.

"Yes, but I would be greatly disappointed and may leave you," she confessed.

"Leave me? But you just said that you'd still love me," he asked, confused by her answer.

"I would still love you. But I would consider leaving," she said.

"Our vows were until death do us part," he countered.

"If you murdered a man, that would tell me you're not the same man anymore, which can only mean that man is dead and gone, leaving me the ability to leave you and have a conscience."

Disturbed by her views, he said, "Let's halt this discussion and agree to disagree."

"Levi?"

"Yes," he said.

"Just don't murder anyone and we don't have to worry about my reaction," she said.

"I'm not going to murder anyone," he shot back.

"Good, now get some sleep, good night," she said.

"Good night," he fired back, his anger slightly risen.

As he lay staring at the ceiling, the slightly lit wick of the lantern cast a glow in the room, enabling him to see. His mind wandered, causing him to contemplate all the events that had occurred since Randall Pritchard had arrived in town. He then found himself wondering if Katherine was telling the truth. Would she really leave him? Was she capable? Was she merely threatening him with the possibility as a deterrent? He came to the conclusion, after knowing her for so long, that she was probably telling him the truth.

SANTA FE, NEW MEXICO TERRITORY

Ted stared out the window, hoping to see his cousin Earl, the only other person that Fester imagined would come to his aid. He and Fester felt confident in their ability to take on Randall, but a third person wielding some iron wouldn't hurt.

Sitting next to him, Fester snored. He slept a lot while traveling, claiming it had to do with the motion of the train.

Ted's eyes scanned the crowd as they slowed to a stop at the expansive depot. When the train came to a full stop, Ted jumped to his feet, smacked Fester on the arm, and barked, "Come on, cousin, let's see if Earl is here."

Fester opened his eyes and looked around. He was a bit disoriented. "Where are we?"

Already making his way down the aisle, pushing past people, Ted replied, "We're in Santa Fe, now c'mon."

Fester got to his feet, stretched and followed Ted. When he climbed down the stairs, he spotted Ted embracing someone; he couldn't tell who it was but assumed it was their cousin. Earl was also a first cousin but from his mother's side. At one time all the families lived in Michigan, but as the West opened up, his uncles and aunts began to migrate with hopes of opportunity and riches. Earl's family settled outside Santa Fe in a gold-mining town called Los Cerrillos.

Seeing Fester walk towards them with his signature crooked smile, Earl broke free from Ted and marched over to him. "Cousin Fester, it's good to see you."

"Earl, you look good, real good," Fester said.

The two men hugged.

Ted bounded over and patted both of them on the shoulder. "Isn't this a scene, the family reunited for one common purpose, get revenge for Ronald."

"My condolences, cousin," Earl said, pulling back from Fester and giving him a once-over. "I see you look well."

"I am, but I'll admit I like the air out here and the dry weather," Fester said.

"There aren't mosquitos here," Earl said.

"How's your ma and pa?" Fester asked.

"They're well, wanted me to pass on their condolences."

"You told them what you're doing?" Fester asked.

"Of course."

"And they're fine with that?" Fester asked.

"Fester, I'm twenty years old. I'm a man; I dictate my own life. I may work in the mines alongside my father, but I do what I want. Plus they all but forced me to go. Pa's big on family and blood, wants us to get revenge for Ronald."

Lowering his head, Ted said, "May he rest in peace."

"The man we're coming up against is a real gunman.

I've mentioned this already to Ted; he's notorious," Fester said.

Earl pulled his coat aside to show his pistol in the holster and pulled a double-barreled shotgun from a scabbard strapped to his back. "You don't need to be a dead shot to hit with this."

"No, you don't," Fester said with a smile.

"Say, when does the train leave?" Ted asked.

"I know what you're asking, and yes, we have time for a whiskey or two," Fester said.

"How about three or four?" Ted asked. For him, he'd never left the farm until now and was making the most of it.

The trio turned and headed for the closest bar or saloon they could find.

CHAPTER SIX

JUNE 15, 1896

PHOENIX, ARIZONA TERRITORY

Levi entered Marshal Clark's office to find the elderly rotund lawman sitting at his desk with his legs propped up, a cigar sticking out of his teeth.

"Ah, Sheriff Bass, did you come to finally tell me what the other night was all about? You know, people are still talking," Clark said as he pulled the cigar from his mouth and exhaled a large plume of smoke in Levi's direction.

Levi wafted through the smoke and took a seat in the small chair at the front of Clark's desk. "I have a couple of questions to ask concerning Brant Stone's death."

"Brant Stone? What the hell do you want to know about him?" Clark asked.

"You might have heard that a man was found hanged near Painted Rock. Well, I've come to discover that the murdered man and Brant Stone were close acquaintances who gambled and drank together."

Clark bellowed loudly, "That's half the damn town, Sheriff. Just because someone knows someone and the two die months apart doesn't mean anything except that."

"Are you sure Stone wasn't murdered?" Levi asked.

"I'm sure. His head was resting on the damn rock he hit coming off his horse. It was a simple accident," Clark replied. "I saw no evidence that he'd been hit with something or that he'd been attacked, just the wound to his head."

"What do you make of the man who was found hanged and Stone knowing each other?"

"Like I said, Sheriff, just because two people know each other and die months apart doesn't mean anything, just dumb luck," Clark answered.

"Do you know who Charlie Torrance is?" Levi asked.

"Yeah, he works for Deveron in Scottsdale," Clark said.

"He's the man we found dangling by his neck. He'd been shot three times too," Levi said.

"Well, that's too bad, poor feller, but it could have been anyone, some rogue Apache or bandit; maybe Charlie was screwing some man's wife and got what was coming to him," Clark said, dismissing the murder as just another crime.

Seeing he was getting nowhere with Clark, Levi nodded then stood up. "Thank you for your time, Marshal."

"So are you gonna admit to me finally what the other night was all about?" Clark again asked. He was relentless in his quest to discover what had driven Levi to act the way he did.

Levi put on his hat and nodded. "Have a good day."

"You too, Sheriff, and remember, my door is always open when you decide to confess your secrets." Clark laughed.

Levi ignored him and exited the office. He shut the door and sighed. He only tolerated Clark; outside of that he couldn't care less about the man. But with his endless questions, his tolerance of him was wearing thin.

"Sheriff, hello, Sheriff!" Randall howled from across the street.

Seeing Randall coming his way, Levi lowered his head and shook it. "Remain calm, Levi," he said to himself.

Randall was on his way to the general store when he spotted Levi. He always found it important to get along with the law in each town and would not rest until he and Levi were on good terms. "Sheriff, how are you doing this fine morning?" Randall asked, offering his hand.

Levi looked at it and asked, "What can I do for you, Mr. Pritchard?"

Pulling his hand back, Randall said, "Sheriff, I just wanted to tell you I'm not who you think I am."

Levi stood staring.

"I've never been somewhere and not had a good relationship with the law. As you know, me and Marshal Clark go way back. That's how my relationships usually are, and I want us to have that."

"Mr. Pritchard, that's not going to happen," Levi said.

"And why's that?" Randall asked.

"On account I don't like your kind," Levi said.

"And what kind is that?"

Feeling his anger well up inside, Levi leaned in and

snarled, "You're a low-down scoundrel, thief and cheat."

Pointing at himself, Randall asked, "I'm a cheat?"

"Mr. Pritchard, I've said my piece. Now get out of my face," Levi barked.

"You're an arrogant ass, aren't you?" Randall snapped. He'd finally reached the limit of his patience with Levi.

"You're calling me an ass?" Levi asked.

The marshal's office door opened and out stepped Clark. "What in the hell is going on? Are you bothering Mr. Pritchard again, Sheriff?"

"Stay out of this, Marshal," Levi fired back.

"I'm fine, Marshal. I'm just informing the sheriff that he's a real ass. You know, one of those righteous ones who talks a big game about how good he is; then you catch him in the barn doing all kinds of vile things to animals."

Levi reached back and touched the back strap of his pistol.

Randall did the same.

"Whoa, whoa, whoa, ease up, now!" Clark howled as he jumped from the walkway down onto the street. He stepped in between the two men, his face towards Levi. "Damn it, Levi, you're the sheriff and you're acting like some sort of gunslinger. The thing is you're not, you're just a simple sheriff, nothing more. Mr. Pritchard back here is quick on the draw, and he'd put a round through you faster than you could break leather."

"Get out of my way, Marshal," Levi seethed.

"Go, leave now!" Clark ordered his left arm raised and pointed down the street. "Walk away now!"

Levi could hear Katherine's voice in his head, yelling

at him to stop. He took his hand off the back strap and said, "Keep him away from me."

"Go!" Clark barked.

Levi glanced over Clark's shoulder and leered at Randall before turning and walking off.

"Anytime, Sheriff, you know where I'm staying," Randall taunted.

Levi stopped but didn't turn around. Randall's words were delivered in the same condescending way he'd done so all those years ago to his father.

"C'mon, Sheriff, let's see what you have," Randall again taunted.

"Randall, shut up!" Clark snapped.

"He's the one who started it, Marshal," Randall protested.

Levi ground his teeth, took a deep breath, and kept walking away. The farther he got, the easier it was to take the next step. Before long he was out in front of the church. He stared at the church, knowing he should go in and talk with Father McKenna. Katherine's voice was still pleading with him for calm serenity. A question popped in his head, and he knew Father McKenna would be the right one to answer it. He turned and headed inside, to see it was filled with ten parishioners, who all were kneeling in random pews scattered around.

"Where's Father McKenna?" Levi asked a parishioner, an elderly woman who was sitting in a pew near the back.

"He's in the sanctum," the woman replied, looking up from her prayer.

Levi headed farther down the aisle towards the altar.

"Levi, is that you?" a booming voice asked from behind him.

Levi recognized the voice. He stopped, craned his head back, and said, "Father McKenna, you're the man I'm here to see."

Father McKenna walked up to Levi with his arms open. "My dear boy, so good to see you."

"Father, it's been a long time, I apologize."

Father McKenna embraced Levi, who didn't return the gesture, and said, "I saw your wife the other day, fine woman; you definitely married up. She said something about you coming to visit me earlier in the week, but I didn't see you."

"I've been busy. Can we talk?" Levi asked, his jawed clenched in an attempt to keep his anger at bay.

"You look a little tense," McKenna said.

"It's been a tough few days," Levi replied.

"I hear a man was murdered, how sad. Is that something you're looking into?" McKenna asked.

Not wanting to answer a litany of questions, Levi cleared his throat and asked, "Father, can we?"

"Of course, of course, come with me," McKenna said, motioning towards the sanctum.

"Actually, Father, I was hoping we could go and *talk*," Levi said, motioning his head in the direction of the confessionals.

McKenna placed his wrinkled hand on Levi' shoulder and said, "You want me to hear your confession. Now I understand. Yes, come, right this way."

Inside the dark and musty confessional, Levi sat and contemplated what he'd say. He blinked repeatedly until his eyes adjusted to the faint light.

McKenna entered his side of the confessional, shifted in his seat, and opened the dividing screen that separated the two men. "Go ahead, my son."

"Father, I'm going to skip the formalities," Levi said.

"That's fine, go ahead," McKenna said.

"Father, does God forgive us for killing our enemies?" Levi asked.

"If you repent, I believe God forgives," McKenna replied.

"Even if we would enjoy it? If we take pleasure in seeing a man get killed?" Levi asked.

McKenna shifted in his seat and leaned closer to the screen and said, "What's in your heart, son?"

"Father, does God believe there is a difference between killing and murder?"

"He has given us his laws, and thou shall not kill is his sixth. However, one can be forgiven if one is truly repentant, but I stress again, what is in your heart is what's important to him. Each life taken is a tragedy, but when the killing is done in the protection of your community, your town or, in your case, in the exercise of your duties, that is just in God's eyes, I've said that before."

"What about in the name of justice?" Levi asked.

"Levi, we are not put on this Earth to judge. That is God's and his alone."

"What if I knew someone had committed a heinous act, but there was no law to arrest him, there was no system to punish him, and the only way to get that justice was to kill him?"

McKenna cleared his throat and asked, "Levi, what are you asking me?"

"Does God view the premeditated killing of someone the same as murder?"

"To seek out one with the sole purpose of killing them is murder, that is wrong in the eyes of God, but all sins can be forgiven. Remember, anyone who believes in the salvation of Jesus Christ can be forgiven, even the murderer."

"So if I murdered someone, I could later receive forgiveness?" Levi asked.

"Yes, but, Levi, you're concerning me. What have you done? Please, son, confess your sins so that you may be absolved. I can hear the pain in your heart."

"It's not pain you're hearing, Father, it's anger," Levi said and stood up to leave. He opened the curtain and said, "Thank you, Father, this little talk has helped."

"Wait, don't leave, please. If you've murdered someone, you need to confess this sin and repent now," McKenna insisted.

"I can't do that," Levi said boldly.

"Why can't you?" McKenna asked.

"Because I haven't murdered him yet," Levi stated then quickly exited the confessional.

***

Still feeling the tinge of anger after his confrontation with

Levi, Randall headed into the general store. Standing at the counter was Savannah, but gone was her normal jovial smile. "Good day, little lady," Randall said.

"Hello," Savannah said, her tone melancholy.

Sensing something was wrong but purposely trying to avoid asking, Randall said, "That perfume did the trick. I even got a kiss for it."

"That's nice, sir," Savannah said.

Dark circles around Savannah's eyes told Randall the poor girl hadn't slept well the night before.

"Can I get another pound of licorice?" Randall asked.

"Yes, sir," Savannah said, picking up the tongs.

Seeing the ring on her finger, he thought he'd ask about her husband to elicit an answer. "What does your husband do?"

She looked up from the jar of licorice and replied, "My husband's dead, died seven weeks ago."

"My condolences," Randall said. "How?"

"Well, I was first told it was an accident. Now it appears he might have been murdered, and why? I'll tell ya 'cause you'll probably ask, and if you don't, you'll be wondering. He was a lying gambler and got what comes to people like him."

"Your husband died when he was gambling?" Randall asked, shocked to hear the specifics of his death.

"The town marshal thought it was an accident, but the county sheriff seems to think it could be murder. You see, he came by last night and asked me a few questions, and it now seems plausible that Brant, he's my husband, was killed for his money or because he owed someone. It breaks my heart, it really does, because he knew how I feel about gambling, yet he did it anyway. And what makes matters worse is he mortgaged our house and land so he could gamble or pay his debts back. Now with him gone, I had to find a job like this just so I don't lose it," she said with tears welling up in her eyes.

"My dear girl, I'm so sorry to hear about your troubles, I truly am," Randall said, wishing he could go behind the counter and give her a big hug.

"I'm sorry too. He brought me all the way to Phoenix so we could have a new start. I always wondered what he meant by that, and now I can see what it means. He probably had to flee Tucson because of his gambling. Now he's dead and I'm on the verge of losing all I have." She groaned.

"Is there anything I can do to help?" Randall asked.

"Why would you help me? I'm no one to you," Savannah said.

"You're someone to somebody, that's for sure, and I'd help because it's what's right," Randall said.

"You're awful nice, but I'm not one for charity. I'd rather work for my living than receive anything for free."

"Please let me help. I can lend you money," Randall offered.

Savannah gave him an odd look and asked, "Why?"

"Like I said," Randall replied.

"Are you hoping to get some advantage on me?" Savannah asked, her tone turning suspicious.

"No, no, nothing like that," Randall answered defensively.

"I'd like to keep our relationship as it is. Now, can I get you anything besides the licorice?" she asked.

Not wanting to press, Randall relented. "A newspaper as well."

She took one from a stack next to him, folded it, and placed it in a sack. She finished packaging the licorice and put them in as well. "Is that all, sir?"

"That'll be fine," Randall said.

"Seventy-five cents," she said.

Randall gave her a dollar coin and said, "Keep the change."

She smiled and said, "Tips I'll accept, thank you."

Randall picked up the sack, tipped his hat, and said, "You have a fine day."

"Good day…um, wait, sir. What's your name?" she asked. "I figure since you know mine and I'll be seeing you more, I should at least address you properly."

Randall froze; he stood and stared.

"You okay, sir, the cat got your tongue?" Savannah asked.

He caught sight of the newspapers in a stack, scanned a few lines, and spotted a name. "Mr. Washington."

Savannah stuck out her hand. "Nice to meet you, Mr. Washington."

Feeling awkward, he took her hand and said, "Nice to meet you too, Savannah." He let go, turned and rushed out of the store. Outside, he took a couple of deep breaths and thought about how he'd felt the instant she asked him his name. That moment was as close as he'd come to revealing himself, yet he couldn't do it; the timing still wasn't right.

His day had started off good with a nice breakfast with Jane but had quickly spiraled downward after meeting the sheriff and now his encounter with Savannah. The poor girl was in trouble, and he had no way of helping her. He needed to, but how? He scurried across the busy street and towards the hotel. If there was one person he could trust in this matter, it was Jane, and he needed to speak with her right away.

***

Randall found Jane in her room knitting, and she was more than willing to lend an ear to his plight. He described Savannah's situation and his offer to her. He detailed how she vehemently refused any help and that she started to become suspicious of his motives. And lastly he told her about the instant she asked him what his name was.

"Mr. Washington?" She laughed. "What's your first name, George?"

"I can see the humor, but it's not funny," Randall shot back, annoyed. "I'm in a pickle here. My daughter needs help in a way I can be helpful, yet I'm powerless."

"Let's go through this. Her now deceased husband mortgaged the house and land. She's behind on the payments because she didn't know about the mortgage, and now she's working a job at the general store to help pay it?"

"Correct."

"I say keep letting her work and give enough money to the owner, Mr. Montgomery, to keep her on. If she wants to pay her own way, let her," Jane said.

"No, I won't allow her to possibly lose her land and her home. After I'm gone, I have no idea if Montgomery will do as I've requested. If she wants to work to make a wage to buy things, that's one thing, but if her home is threatened…no, I've got to find a way to pay off her mortgage for her."

"You've just found the solution right there," Jane said, her small frame perched in the cushioned chair in the corner of the room.

Randall stopped pacing and asked, "I did?"

"Go to the bank and pay it off," Jane said.

"I can do that?" Randall asked, confused about the process.

"Haven't you ever bought a piece of land or a house and needed money?" Jane asked.

"I'm rich, Jane. No, I've never needed a mortgage. If I want something, I simply buy it with cash," Randall said.

"The bank doesn't care where the money comes from. Go to the bank where the note is and pay it off," Jane said.

"It's that easy?" Randall asked, still not understanding.

"Yes, Randall, it's that easy. I can go with you if you like," she said.

"No, that won't be necessary," he said. As he thought about how easy the solution was, he turned to focus on when and if he should reveal himself to her. "I didn't tell you, but I woke this morning in a lot of pain. The cancer is progressing, getting worse; I don't know how long I have, yet I can't find the words or the right timing to tell her I am her father."

"You're a big, strong man; the perfect timing might not ever show itself, so find the courage to just go to her one day and simply tell her. Make no demands of her, pass no judgments on her past behavior towards you; just tell her who you are and that you love her," Jane said.

"Shouldn't I tell her I want to see her and that I want her with me when I die? I really want her by my bedside when I take my last breath," he said.

"Make no demands of her, you can't; you lost that right when you left," Jane said.

"But I left because her mother demanded I leave. I left for her," Randall replied.

"You're making this about you; it has to be about her," Jane countered.

"But I'm the one dying. She needs to see me," Randall insisted, his ears closed to Jane's words.

"You're still making it about you. Why do you want to see her? Is it because you feel guilty? Is it because of what you want? Or are you doing so for her so that she can later on in life look back on her father and have a tinge of pride or love?"

Randall thought as he paced.

"It has to be about what your intention is," Jane said.

"My intention is to reconnect with her, let her know how much I love her, and that for every day I was gone, I missed her and thought about her; that I didn't leave because I didn't want her, I left because her mother thought it best, and later on I agreed with that. Jane, I'm a gambler; I've killed men. When I look back on my life, I'm not a good man," Randall said. He could feel the pull of gravity on his legs. He walked to the edge of the bed and sat down.

"I think you're a good man who over his life made bad choices over and over again. I don't think you're evil, just flawed, and now you seem to want redemption. You should start with yourself, then with God, and only then can you go to her and seek it," Jane said.

"You're right. I don't forgive myself for those years I was gone," he said.

"If you want her to forgive you, you first need to forgive yourself," she said, getting up and walking over to him. She placed her hands tenderly on his shoulders and continued, "Don't force this. Make amends with your own past; then we'll talk about how you can approach her."

"I must have done something right in my life to have you in it for my last days," Randall said, looking up into her eyes.

"Like I said, we were meant to meet," Jane said and gave him a kiss on the lips.

***

Katherine watched in horror as Levi gathered her clothing and tossed it in a trunk. Repeatedly he went to her wardrobe and dresser, scooped up an armful, walked back to the trunk, and threw it in.

"Levi, stop! You need to tell me what's going on!" she exclaimed.

Zeke walked into the open doorway. "I'm packed, Pa."

Levi looked up and said, "Good boy."

Katherine walked up to Levi, grabbed him by the shoulders, and stopped him. "Talk to me. What's going on?"

"I told you, I'm sending you ahead to Prescott. I'll follow soon," he said.

"Is this about that murder?" she asked, fear in her cracking voice.

"It's just unsafe, that's all I can say," Levi replied.

"Unsafe?"

"Pa, is someone trying to kill us?"

"Zeke, go gather what you'll need from the pantry for the trip," Levi ordered.

Ever obedient, Zeke raced off.

"Levi, stop this now! Talk to me!" Katherine blared, her emotions running high.

"Katherine, there's no time to discuss this. I have you and Zeke on the evening coach to Prescott. I'll follow in a week or so," Levi lied. He wasn't sure when he'd meet up with them if ever. He'd made up his mind, he was going to kill Randall, but he was going to be smart about it. Get his family out of harm's way and ensure his finances were set as well as his will and testament just in case he didn't survive the ordeal.

Katherine began to weep.

He wiped her tears and said softly, "I don't know what will happen. I just want to make sure you and Zeke are safe."

"Are the murderers coming after you now? Have they threatened us?" Katherine asked.

THE RETRIBUTION OF LEVI BASS

"All you need to know is once you're out of town and on the road to Prescott, you'll be safe," Levi said.

Loud banging came from the front door below.

Katherine cried out in fear, "Is that them? Are they here to kill us?"

Levi raced from the room, stopped at the top of the stairs, and called down to Zeke, "Get on up here!"

"Levi, I'm scared," Katherine said, walking up behind him.

Zeke ran up the stairs and into Katherine's arms.

"Sheriff, it's Deputy Thompson. I've got some important news."

Katherine breathed a sigh of relief.

Levi ran down the stairs, jumping a couple as he went, unlocked the door, and flung it open. "What is it?"

"One of the fellas we're seeking, Al, he's in the Desert Rose Bar, drunk as a skunk and talking a big game," Thompson said.

Levi grabbed his hat, turned back to Katherine, and said, "Finish getting packed. If I don't come back, head to the Overland Stage station at four o'clock. There are two tickets there for you and Zeke on the four-thirty coach."

She nodded and said, "I love you, Levi, and be safe; come back to us."

He nodded and exited out the door. It tore him up inside to be lying to her, but if he was going to exact his revenge on Randall, he couldn't risk having her around.

Thompson and Levi rode as fast as their horses would take them to the bar. They hopped off, hitched the horses to a post, and headed inside.

The Desert Rose was one of the rowdier bars in Phoenix. It was small, housing only four tables, which always seemed to be full. The bar in the corner was L shaped and was as full as the tables, men leaning or perched on it.

Levi turned to Thompson and asked, "Which one is he?"

"He's the loud fella in the back," Thompson said, motioning with a tip of his head.

Levi looked and through the smoky air spotted a short and ugly man. His hair hung down beyond his shoulders and was greasy. When he laughed, his mouth would open wide, showing all the teeth he was missing. A thick scar spanned his right cheek and showed through his heavy stubble. His forehead and nose were covered in dirt and grime, highlighting that he and a bar of soap hadn't been acquainted for some time. By his mannerisms and slurred speech, it was apparent he was heavily intoxicated.

"You should have seen the look on that dumb son of a bitch's face when I pulled my Colt on him!" Al hollered, ripping his pistol from his holster and waving it around.

The men gathered close to him were clearly not impressed, with several telling him to calm down.

"You shut it, or I'll stick this up your ass!" Al barked back. He holstered his pistol, turned towards the bar, and shouted, "Give me another bottle!"

"Stay here. I'll go get him," Levi ordered.

"You sure?" Thompson asked.

"Watch over me, be ready, but let me take him," Levi said confidently. He took a deep breath and focused on Al.

He weaved through the crowd until he was in front of Al.

Al looked at him but didn't look down to see his badge. "Who the hell are you?"

"Have you seen Samuel?" Levi asked.

"What about him?" Al mumbled as he swayed back and forth, his greasy hair getting caught in the thick stubble on his chin.

"I hear he's in trouble," Levi said.

Al smirked and gave Levi a second look, this time glancing down to see his badge. He blinked hard and leaned in to get a closer look. "Oh, hell, you're the damn sheriff."

"That I am," Levi said, ripping his pistol from his holster. He cocked back and smacked Al in the face with the butt of the grip.

Al's head snapped back. He stumbled backwards, stopping only when he hit the wall. A streak of blood streamed down his face from the cut on his forehead. "You hit me," he groaned. He reached back for his pistol.

Levi stepped forward and again struck him with the butt of his pistol, this time striking him on the jaw.

Al's eyes rolled back into his head, and he dropped to the floor like a heavy sack of potatoes, hitting the floor with a pronounced thud.

The crowd in the bar, which had turned quiet upon the encounter, erupted into a raucous cheer.

"Sheriff, you just did the public a service!" the bartender howled.

Levi smiled at the bartender, spun around, and hollered, "Thompson, let's get him to the office pronto.

I've got some questions I need answered."

***

Taking Jane's advice, Randall went directly to the bank. He entered the building and saw nothing but teller windows. He walked up to one and said, "I need to speak with someone about a mortgage."

The young clerk manning the window looked up, smiled and said, "Mr. Sullivan can help you with that. If you give me just a moment, sir, I'll notify him that you're here. Who do I say is needing the assistance?"

"My name is Randall Pritchard."

The teller's eyes widened and his brow furrowed. "The Mr. Pritchard, the gambler?"

"That would be me," Randall replied.

"How exciting to have someone of your status in the bank. Let me notify Mr. Sullivan," the teller said then rushed off.

Moments later a side door opened, and there stood Mr. Sullivan, his wire spectacles clinging to the bridge of his nose. "Mr. Pritchard, it's a pleasure to have you at the First Arizona Building and Trust."

Randall walked up and said, "Thank you for seeing me so quickly."

Sullivan stepped out of the way and motioned with his arm. "Right this way, sir. My desk is just there. Please take a seat in the chair next to it."

Randall did as he said.

Sullivan briskly went to his seat, cleared a file from the

desk, and asked, "Now, are you buying a property, or do you need money and want to use a piece of land as collateral?"

"Mrs. Stone, does she have a mortgage here?"

"Are you referring to Mrs. Stone, the widow?" Sullivan asked, a look of confusion on his face.

"That would be the one," Randall said.

"Sir, we're not at liberty to discuss other clients' accounts, but I'm more than happy to process an application for you," Sullivan said.

"I'm here to pay off her mortgage. How much is it?" Randall asked, getting right to the point.

Flabbergasted, Sullivan sat back in his chair and asked, "You've come to pay off her mortgage?"

"Yes, the entire amount. How much is it?" Randall asked.

"Forgive me if I'm a bit stupefied. We normally don't get people coming in to pay off a stranger's debt," Sullivan said.

"Can I do it or not?" Randall asked.

Sullivan thought for a moment and replied, "I don't see why not."

"Then how much is it?" Randall asked.

Sullivan pushed his chair away from the desk, stood and said, "I'll be right back. Let me go get the file." Sullivan rushed away.

Randall could hear a hushed conversation taking place just outside the office door.

Sullivan reappeared, this time with a file folder in his grasp. He sat down, opened it up, and read. "She owes seven hundred and sixty-two dollars."

Randall didn't flinch; he removed a long leather wallet from his inner coat pocket, opened it, and thumbed through the bills. He removed a small stack of bills and set them on the desk. "That's seven hundred and sixty dollars." He reached into his trouser pocket, fished around, and pulled out a few coins. He set two down and said, "That makes seven sixty-two."

Still bewildered by why Randall would be doing such a thing, Sullivan asked, "Are you sure you want to be doing something like this?"

"I'm quite sure. As a matter of fact, I'd also like to open a savings account under her name."

"You would?"

"Yes."

"Very well," Sullivan said. "Do you want to be a cosigner?"

"No, just an account under her name," Randall said.

Taking a pad of paper next to him, Sullivan jotted down a few notes. "And how much would you like to deposit into this account for Mrs. Stone?"

Randall pulled the remaining cash from his wallet and set it in front of Sullivan. "However much that is."

Sullivan stared at the large sum of money and asked, "This?"

"Yes."

Sullivan counted it, and when he finished, he said, "That's two thousand, four hundred and twenty-one dollars. Mr. Pritchard, are you sure you want to be doing this for Mrs. Stone? Has she made you promises of some sort?"

"No, she hasn't, and I need you to keep these transactions confidential," Randall said.

"Of course, mum is the word," Sullivan said.

Randall waited as Sullivan prepared all the paperwork and returned with it for Randall to sign. "Just sign here for the receipt of funds and also sign here acknowledging you gave the money to pay her mortgage balance."

Randall happily signed. After setting down the pen, he smiled and said, "That felt really good."

"I'm sure it did. And I'm sure Mrs. Stone is going to be thrilled when she finds out," Sullivan said.

"Mr. Sullivan, if that's it, I'll be going," Randall said, getting to his feet.

Sullivan followed suit and stuck his hand out. "Pleasure doing business with you."

The two men shook hands.

"Mr. Sullivan, do you have an attorney whom you could refer me to?" Randall asked.

"Yes, go see Mr. William Gibbs. He's a fine and trustworthy attorney. I use him personally," Sullivan said.

"Thank you and have a good day," Randall said. He turned and exited.

As he left the bank, Randall felt better than when he went in. He had given her the one gift he could give, and even if she never knew who her benefactor was, he was fine with it. As long as she was taken care of, that was all he cared about.

***

Jane sped across the street to avoid the wagon barreling towards her. Stopping just outside Montgomery's General Store, she took as deep a breath as she could, something that was getting harder and harder to accomplish these days and was no doubt a sign of her worsening condition. Clearing her throat after a couple of raspy coughs, she climbed onto the walkway and stepped into the store.

Hearing the bell ring, signaling someone had entered the store, Savannah called out from the storeroom, "Good day." She walked out to see Jane at the counter. "Hello, how may I help you?"

"I heard Mr. Montgomery buys valuables," Jane said.

"He does. Let me go get him," Savannah said, walking back into the storeroom.

Seconds later Montgomery appeared. "Hello there."

"Hi, I heard you buy valuables like jewelry," Jane said.

"I do."

"Good," Jane said, opening a small clutch and removing a necklace, two broaches and a ring. "I have these I'd like to sell. The broaches were given to me by my mother, who received them from her mother in Europe. Hard to believe they made it all the way from England."

Montgomery slid the jewelry closer and put his spectacles on the tip of his nose. He carefully examined them and said, "I'll give you ten dollars for all of it."

"Ten dollars?" Jane asked, shocked.

"I'm not really in need of more things, as you can see," he said, pointing to a glass-covered case. Inside were dozens of items all lined in rows.

"I see, but can you do better? That broach there has a ruby in it, and that necklace has an emerald as the center stone."

"I'll tell you what, I'll give you thirteen," he said.

Jane chewed on the side of her cheek as she thought.

Savannah gave Jane a sympathetic look, as she wasn't the only one going through tough financial times.

"If you want, I can set them aside for you to buy back if you're just needing the money for short term," Montgomery said.

"I won't be needing them back," Jane said.

Montgomery collected the jewelry and placed them on a counter behind him and removed thirteen dollars from the cash drawer. "Here you go," he said, handing her the cash.

Jane took the money, folded it over once, and shoved it into her clutch. "Thank you."

"You're very welcome. Please tell anyone you know that I buy as well as sell," he said.

"I'll be sure to do that," Jane said.

"Take care," Montgomery said and headed back to the storeroom.

Jane turned to leave but was stopped when Savannah called out, "Ma'am, I'm sorry you had to sell your beautiful jewelry."

Jane spun around, smiled and said, "It's only material possessions. I won't be needing them soon anyway."

"Are you going somewhere?" Savannah asked.

"If I have my way, it'll be heaven," Jane said with a

blissful smile.

"Oh dear, forgive me; I didn't know you were sick," Savannah said, her expression displaying shock.

"If there's one thing that's certain in life, it's death; we're all going to die one day," Jane said.

"You're so upbeat for someone who knows that death is knocking on their door," Savannah said, curious as to how she could be content.

"My dear, life is hard, it just is. There was a German philosopher by the name of Friedrich Nietzsche, and he said, forgive me if the quote is wrong, but something along the line that life is suffering. Once we come to grips with that, it makes life much easier to live. Just remove the expectation that life will be pleasant and you'll be happier, I promise."

Savannah thought about what she said, then replied, "That's wise."

"I've lived by those words as well as other great philosophers, and they've served me. I also believe that whom we have in our lives isn't an accident, and what happens to us is all part of a larger plan, that they're teachable moments," Jane said.

"Can I share something with you?" Savannah asked, drawing closer to Jane.

"Of course," Jane answered.

"My husband recently passed away. I've come now to discover that he might have been murdered and that he also lied. Are you saying that was all meant to happen, that there's a reason for that?"

"Yes and no, yes, that life shows up and there are

lessons you can learn from every experience. Remember, it's your choice how you respond to it. God has a plan for you, and you're here to learn. And no, in that you didn't have a direct connection to the event happening. You're not responsible for what your husband did or for his death; that was his choice."

"I'm sorry, that all sounds very complicated," Savannah said.

"It's okay, dear; it took me a while to understand it all too," Jane said. "And let me also say that I'm sorry for your loss."

"It was a shock," Savannah said.

"I've heard you're a strong person. I think you'll be okay," Jane said. "Now, I should be going. Have a wonderful day."

"Excuse me," Savannah said, again stopping Jane.

"Yes," Jane said.

"What did you mean you heard I was a strong person?" Savannah asked.

Stunned by the question and regretful she'd slipped up, Jane replied, "Oh, I think I heard someone mention you, a friend of mine."

"No one knows me. I find that hard to believe," Savannah said, getting suspicious.

"I wish you well," Jane said, ignoring Savannah's last comment. She turned and headed for the door.

"Do you know Mr. Washington? Is that the connection?" Savannah said.

Jane reached the door and stopped.

"Did he send you in here? Because if he did, I don't

appreciate him sharing the details of my life with strangers. As a matter of fact, he's a stranger and I question his motives."

Jane turned around and said, "The motives you're really questioning are your dead husband's. I know that sounds like a harsh judgment, but you are, and you're transferring that onto people who wish to help you."

"I don't know what you two want, but I don't need anything from anyone. Please tell him that," Savannah said.

Unable to resist, Jane headed back towards Savannah. "Randall is a good man. His intentions are honorable."

"Randall?"

Jane growled under her breath once she realized she'd given up Randall's name to her.

Savannah shook her head and said, "Randall is my father's name."

"It's just a coincidence. Many people have similar names," Jane said, hoping to deflect.

Montgomery came from the storeroom and blared, "I can't stand this back-and-forth anymore. Would you and Mr. Pritchard please stop these antics."

"Pritchard?" Savannah said, her face turning white.

Jane grunted her displeasure.

"Mr. Washington is my father, Randall Pritchard? That man was my father?" Savannah asked, bewildered by the revelation.

"I wasn't aware that he was your father, but he is Randall Pritchard, the famous gambler," Montgomery said.

Knowing she needed to rectify the situation quickly, Jane approached Savannah. "Please listen to me. He's a good man who's made poor choices, but he loves you and only wishes to see you. He means no harm, none whatsoever."

"He lied to me; you lied to me," Savannah said, her shock turning to anger.

"He only wishes to see you, to get to know you," Jane rattled off.

"If he wanted to get to know me, he should have stayed in my life and not abandoned me and my mother," Savannah roared, her anger reaching a crescendo.

Seeing he'd whipped up a hornet's nest, Montgomery turned and went back to the storeroom.

"Your mother told him to leave, he protested, but she told him to stay away. He wanted to see you, he did, but after time went by, he began to believe that his influence was exactly as your mother said it was."

"He left me when I was a baby," Savannah snapped.

"Not true, he was with you until you were three; then he left," Jane said, bringing forward her best defense.

"You're lying. My mother told me he left after I was born. He abandoned us," Savannah said.

"No, dear, he left when you were three at the request of your mother. She wanted him gone; she didn't want a gambler living in her house and raising you."

"You're lying!" Savannah screamed.

"Please, Savannah, I need you to listen. All he wants to do is apologize for the past and to see you. He has no demands of you; he wants nothing," Jane pleaded.

"No demands? He wants to see me; that's a demand. He came in here under false pretenses. He's the same as he's always been, a cheat and a liar," Savannah cried.

"I can tell you that he's a good man, just imperfect like we all are," Jane said.

"Leave and tell my father not to come around here anymore," Savannah barked.

"Savannah, please let me explain," Jane begged.

Pointing towards the front door, Savannah ordered, "Leave now!"

Knowing she'd failed miserably, Jane grew quiet. She turned and headed for the door. She opened it, but before she left, she said, "He loves you very much. Please reconsider and see him before he dies."

Tears ran down Savannah's face. The past weeks had been emotionally taxing, and now she was presented with another emotional albatross hung around her neck. Unable to control her anger, she screamed, "Out!"

Jane opened the door and exited. She closed the door softly and looked towards the hotel. All she could think was what Randall would say once he heard she'd accidentally given away his identity to Savannah. Would he listen and forgive? Or would he be angry and cast her out? Knowing she needed to tell him sooner rather than later, she sped towards the hotel and towards a conversation she dreaded having.

***

Levi sat in his chair and stared at Al lying unconscious in the jail cell.

Thompson had just left to go get food for the two.

He looked up at the clock and saw that it was only one o'clock. He knew he needed to go home and check on Katherine, but he was anxious to hear what Al had to say. He knew there was more to the murder of Charlie Torrance and believed that Brant Stone's death might be linked.

The door opened and he assumed it was Thompson, but when he heard Katherine's voice, he sprang from the chair and turned to see her coming towards him.

"I just spoke with Father McKenna," Katherine howled.

"What?"

"I just spoke with Father McKenna, and he told me everything. He was concerned for you and told me every single word."

"That's supposed to be privileged," Levi replied.

She marched up to within inches and, with her finger pointed in his face, said, "You lied. You wanted us gone so you could murder that man. How dare you? How dare you do something so reckless, so…I'm so angry with you right now!"

Knowing he'd never be able to explain, he decided to tell her the truth. "I encountered Pritchard on the street this morning. He wanted to talk, but it's best I stay away from him. He wouldn't leave me alone. I was having a hard time controlling my temper. The next thing that happened was he got mad too, and then he started in on me, just like he did to my father."

"Enough, your father was a drunk and he alone killed your mother and shot you. This has nothing to do with that man. He's just a pawn in your inability to deal with your past. You feel the need to blame someone, so you've chosen him. What you never expected was that you'd run into him. Now you've got yourself lathered up. That man hasn't done a thing; he was just at the right place at the right time. Your father walked into that saloon seeking him out."

"You don't understand," Levi said.

"I understand that you've lost your senses and you've broken my heart; you wanted me and Zeke to leave, well, we are, but not to Prescott. We're going to Tucson on the train today. We'll be headed to my uncle's ranch. When you think you're ready to be a husband and father, come and get us, but not before, and if you're going to kill that man, then don't ever come."

"Katherine, please don't do this. Just wait, we can talk more later," Levi begged.

"You did this. No one made you. You alone made the decision to pack us up so you could have some blood revenge against an innocent man. And let me say this so you don't get it in your head that I'm on his side. I don't think that he's a good man; he's just a man who happened to be there when your father came along. Did he taunt him? I'm sure he did, but your father chose how he reacted to it, and he did what he did, not that gambler."

Levi stepped towards her.

"No, stay away from me. Take this time and think about what you want; you're in control of your own fate, and if it's to kill that man, then do so, but know you'll never see me or Zeke again," Katherine threatened.

"Katherine, please let me explain," Levi said.

"There's nothing to explain. I've heard the story about your father and that night. I never agreed with you that that man was to blame, but you kept casting all responsibility on him. I never thought much of it because I never imagined he'd show up in Phoenix and you'd lose your wits, yet here we are," she blared. Frustrated and angry, she turned and marched back to the front door. She grabbed the knob and opened the door, but before she left, she said, "Levi, I do love you, but I won't let you be a part of my and Zeke's life if you go through with this plan of yours. So if you change your mind and want to be a family again, you know where to find us." She walked through the open door and shut it behind her.

Levi almost toppled to the ground. The pain he felt ran through his body. He'd made the biggest blunder in his life, but his one saving grace was that Katherine gave him one chance to correct it. It was as simple as killing Randall or keeping his family; he couldn't have both. He had planned on getting them out of town then plotting to have Randall taken out. With Father McKenna telling Katherine his confession, he couldn't go forward. He was boxed in and presented a simple choice, family or Randall, and of course he'd choose his family.

"Well, Sheriff, you've got yourself in a spot with your wife." Al chuckled.

Levi spun around and saw Al sitting up, his back against the wall, laughing.

"Good, you're awake," Levi said, shifting gears. One way to put his mind at ease was to work, and Al presented him with just that.

"Where's Samuel?" Al asked. "You mentioned him in the bar."

Levi walked over to the cell and asked, "Why did you kill Charlie Torrance?"

"Who?"

"If you help me, I'll make sure the judge is lenient on your sentence, but you'll need to cooperate," Levi said.

"I don't know a Charlie Torrance," Al spat.

"And where is your compatriot Samuel?" Levi asked.

Al stood up and went to the bars closest to Levi and said, "You told me you knew where he was."

"I lied."

"Figures, you lawmen are liars and criminals with badges."

"Since you're not willing to confess or cooperate, I'll just leave you here while I go tell Mr. Deveron we have the man who killed his man Charlie."

"I didn't kill anyone named Charlie. Heck, I haven't killed a soul. I'm a God-fearing man," Al said.

"Mr. Deveron liked Charlie and so did his other friends. I'm sure they'll ride over with a mob with hopes they can lynch you, and you know something, I think when they arrive, I'll step out, maybe go to the saloon. This will give them a chance to talk to you...privately," Levi said.

"You wouldn't do that," Al said.

"How much of that conversation did you hear with my wife?" Levi asked.

"All of it," Al replied.

"Then you know that I'm a man who will do anything,

including a plot to murder a man, so don't doubt me."

Al walked back to his cot and sat down.

"I'll give you one last chance. Where is Samuel, and why did you kill Charlie Torrance?"

"You'll prevent them from lynching me?" Al asked.

"I won't let a soul in here; no one will touch you. You'll get a fair trial, and I'll talk to the judge about giving you leniency."

"What does that mean?"

"Probably jail instead of getting hanged," Levi answered. "But you'll need to give me verifiable information and place all the blame on your friend, you know the story, he made you do it. It was all his idea."

Al jumped up from the cot and rushed to the side of his cell. "It was all his idea, all of it. It was his plan from the start all the way back."

"Did you all kill Brant Stone?" Levi asked.

"It was Samuel," Al answered.

"And Charlie Torrance?"

"All Samuel."

"You mentioned a plan, what was that?" Levi asked. He was quite happy that it didn't take much to get Al to talk.

"Samuel had this plan. He'd find these young gamblers, play them and lose; he'd then tell them he wanted to raise the stakes, big stakes, thousands of dollars. Some didn't buy the story, but Stone and Charlie did. When we knew they had their money, the plan was to simply rob them, but Samuel took it too far with Stone and killed him. The same thing happened with Charlie. I didn't have anything to do with it; it was all Samuel."

"And where's Samuel now?" Levi asked.

"He's planning on robbing Mr. Pritchard. He knew he'd never buy his story, so he was planning to rob him. We know where he sleeps, and the plan is to break in late tonight and take his money," Al confessed.

"Where can I find him?" Levi asked.

"There's a shack outside town, just about a mile off the Scottsdale road near where you found Charlie. He's staying there," Al replied.

"And what were you doing at the bar?" Levi asked.

"I went into town today to make sure Pritchard was still here. I was supposed to return, but you showed up, and here I am," Al said.

A devious idea popped in Levi's head for a brief moment. He could just allow Samuel to go through with his plan and possibly kill Randall, but with Katherine so adamant about Randall not being killed, even if it wasn't him, Katherine might assume it was. He needed to stop Samuel from robbing Randall, and the first thing he had to do was warn the very man he had wanted to kill.

***

Randall found Mr. Gibbs' office and walked in. The office was very small, only large enough to hold a desk, two chairs and a file cabinet.

A man wearing thick round glasses sat at the desk, a pen in his hand. He looked up, removed his glasses, and gave Randall a squint as he pondered who might be visiting him. "Yes."

"Are you Mr. Gibbs?" Randall asked.

"I am, I am. How can I be of service this fine day?" Gibbs asked.

Smiling, Randall said, "It is a fine day, isn't it?"

"Why, it is. Now what can I do for you?"

Randall liked Gibbs instantly. His cheerful demeanor and pleasant smile made him feel at ease. "I need a last will and testament."

"Then you came to the right place. Please have a seat," Gibbs said.

Randall took the chair closest to the only window.

"If you'll just give me a moment, let me get something to take notes on," Gibbs said as he shuffled the papers on his desk into a neat pile and set them in a drawer.

Randall took the moment to look around the space. On the wall behind Gibbs' desk were two framed documents, one a copy of his undergraduate degree from Yale University and the second was his law degree, also from Yale.

Slapping a leather-bound book on the desk and opening it to a marked page, Gibbs said, "I'll ask a series of questions to first get the information that I need, so bear with me. I do this to make sure I don't forget any pertinent details."

"Go ahead," Randall said.

"Name?"

"Randall Sherman Pritchard."

Gibbs stopped writing and lifted his head. "Are you the Randall Pritchard everyone is talking about?"

"Are people talking about me?" Randall quipped.

"I've read about you and your exploits in the papers," Gibbs said with a smile.

"Don't believe everything you read in the papers," Randall joked.

"You're quite the gambler. Tell me, do you play anything else besides five-card draw?"

"It's my preferred game, but I've been known to wager on just about anything. I once made a bet on a pig race."

"A pig race? I didn't know there was anything of the sort."

"Friend, I've traveled all across this big beautiful land, and I've found one thing is constant, and that is people will wager on anything."

"Interesting," Gibbs said.

"It's an uncanny story, but on my way to Kansas City years ago, I stopped in Lawrence. Nice enough town, but the people are wound a bit tight. I had the hardest time finding a good place to play, and expressed my frustration. Well, the bartender told me about a pig race that's held just outside town. He said it was a big affair. I decided to go see what the fuss was, and let me tell you, that bartender was wrong; it wasn't a big affair, it was a huge affair. There must have been a hundred people there. Now I knew I was at the right spot, not because of the crowd but because of the smell. I saunter up, watch a few of these hogs run, and just knew I needed to put some money down. Now it's known I win a lot at gambling; here's why. I study."

"Study, like read books about it?" Gibbs said,

enthralled with Randall's story.

"No, not like that at all. I have a way of reading people and things. I don't know where it came from, but I've had it most of my life. When I'm sitting at a table with several men, I have a good idea of whom I'm playing and if I'll win. Well, the same went for these damn pigs. I walked over to the pen and looked at them. I watched how they interacted with each other, you name it. I saw this one, lean, smaller than the others, and spotted almost like one of those spotted white dogs. I can't remember the name of the breed."

"Dalmatians."

"Yes, that's them. Anyway, I just knew that pig was a winner. I found the man whom I'd make the wager with and put down three hundred on Elmer. Yes, the pig's name was Elmer. And guess what happened?"

"You won!" Gibbs exclaimed.

"No, I lost. Turns out I don't know how to read pigs." Randall laughed.

"Oh no. Did you bet on any more?" Gibbs asked.

"No, I kept watching to learn, but I didn't quite know how to read those damn creatures. I figured they're best served on my plate versus making me money in a hoof race," Randall joked.

"That's a great story," Gibbs said. "You should write these down, preserve them for history."

"Nah, who wants to read about the exploits of a gambler?"

"I told you I'd read about you anytime I saw an article in the paper that featured you," Gibbs said.

"I suppose I just don't rightly care about such stuff anymore. Maybe when I was younger, but now I only care about a few things," Randall said.

Both men sat silent for a moment.

"Shall we begin again?" Gibbs asked.

"Fire away," Randall said.

Gibbs ran through a series of typical questions only to pause when he came to the beneficiaries. "Mrs. Stone, the widow, is your daughter?"

"She is, and I expect you to keep quiet about that," Randall said.

"Of course, of course, I'm obliged to by law. It's called attorney-client privilege," Gibbs said. "Well, isn't that something. She must be proud of you."

"*Proud* isn't a word I'd use to describe how she feels about me," Randall said.

"Oh," Gibbs said, sensing their relationship was strained. "And will Mrs. Stone be receiving all of your estate?"

Randall thought for a moment and said, "That's it. She gets everything."

"Very good. If you'll just let me draft this up properly, I'll have it ready for you to sign by the end of the day at the earliest," Gibbs said.

"Thank you," Randall said.

Gibbs hopped to his feet. "Mr. Pritchard, the pleasure was all mine." He stuck his hand out.

Randall shook it and said, "I'll be back around later so we can finalize it."

"Thank you for putting your legal matters and trust in

me," Gibbs said happily.

Randall nodded and left the office. Outside, he glanced around at the people coming and going about their day. He wondered if any of them were dying like him and were also making their final arrangements. Feeling accomplished and proud that he'd gotten so much done, he decided he deserved to reward himself with a few hands of poker and a glass of whiskey.

**

Finding her strength to tell Randall, Jane went into the dining hall, where he had been for hours gambling.

Seeing her walk in, Randall tossed his cards into the center of the table and said, "I'm out." He got up from the table and headed towards her. "Aren't you a sight for sore eyes?"

Jane gave him a smile and asked, "Can we talk somewhere privately?"

Sensing something was terribly wrong, he asked, "Is everything okay? Is it one of your boys?"

"No."

"Shall I call a doctor?" he asked, walking her over to a chair in the lobby.

"Can we go to my room and talk? There's something I need to tell you," she said.

He nodded.

The two went upstairs and into her room. After she closed the door, he asked, "You're worrying me. What could possibly be wrong?"

Not wanting to wait any longer, Jane just said what was wrong. "She knows."

"Who knows?" he asked, confused about what she was talking about.

"Savannah, she knows who you are. She knows Mr. Washington is you," Jane said.

Randall gritted his teeth and spat, "That damn fool Montgomery must have told her. I'll wring his skinny neck. I told him not to say anything. He's gone and fouled everything up." He headed for the door. "In fact, I'm going to go over there now and give him a piece of my mind."

"It was me," Jane confessed, not wanting to implicate Mr. Montgomery, who had verified Randall's identity.

Randall stopped. He turned and asked, "What do you mean it was you?"

"I told her, but it was accidental," Jane replied. She stepped up to him and touched his arm. "I inadvertently said something."

"What did you say?" he asked, his tone turning angry.

"It doesn't matter how it happened, just know I didn't mean to, but when she heard, I was there defending you. I told her that you love her and want to see her, that you want nothing from her."

"And what did she say?" Randall asked.

"She's processing; give it a day," Jane said, skirting around Savannah's response.

"Jane, what did she say?"

"She told me to leave."

"Jane, I'll ask one more time."

"She said she didn't want to see you…ever," Jane

answered, her body tensing up.

He stewed on the development but found it impossible to control his temper. "You knew I was planning on revealing my identity to her later. I wanted her to get to know me as a warm and nice gentleman before I told her."

"It wouldn't have worked. She's very angry with you over what she thinks happened. I told her she was wrong, that you didn't abandon them, that you were told to leave by her mother, but she wouldn't hear any of it."

"What were you thinking, Jane?" Randall asked.

"I didn't do it on purpose. It was a small verbal misstep, and she picked up on it," Jane said.

Randall began to pace the room.

She went up to him again and placed her hands gently on his chest. "Please don't be angry. We can work this out, I just know it."

"We? No, no, no, you've already fouled this up. You probably went in there chatting away, giving pep talks, and suddenly blurted it out. Jane, you have single-handedly destroyed my chances to meet my daughter, to find some sort of redemption. Why would you do that?"

"I didn't go in there to talk to her. I went there for something else," Jane said defensively.

"But you still went in there, and when you left, she knew, she knew, damn it."

"Please don't raise your voice. I don't like that," she said.

"Well, I don't like you interfering in my personal affairs and throwing them into chaos. I just went to the bank today and met with Mr. Sullivan, the bank manager. He let me pay off her debts, but now she'll know it was me, and knowing her, she'll refuse the money. This is all wrong. Why did you tell her, why?"

"I didn't do it on purpose, I told you that. I didn't mean for her to know, please know that," she said.

He recoiled from her touch and started pacing again. "Why?"

"Randall, there's a way we can fix this, I know it," Jane said, hoping to calm him down so they could talk about finding solutions.

"Jane, you've done enough. I don't need your help," he barked then went for the door.

"Randall, don't go away mad, please. We can find a way to fix this," Jane pleaded. The strain on her body from the argument stimulated a tickle in her chest, which turned to a cough.

He stopped when he heard her begin to hack, but was so filled with anger that he dismissed it and left the room.

Overcome with a coughing fit, she sat on the bed and hacked uncontrollably until blood appeared. She tried to cover her mouth with her hand, but each time she coughed deeply, more blood came up. She pulled her hand back to see it covered. It dripped from her palm and landed on her dress. Distressed, she went to the vanity, took a towel, and pressed it against her face and coughed into it. Tears streamed down her face. She'd messed things up for Randall and so wanted to find a way to heal the wounds she'd opened up.

Randall stood outside and listened to her cough. A

part of him wanted to go back in and comfort her, but he resisted and let his anger win. Needing to get back to the one thing that was constant, he marched downstairs and to the poker table.

SANTA FE, NEW MEXICO TERRITORY

Fester, Ted and Earl finally boarded the train headed to Phoenix. What was supposed to have been a one-hour delay had turned into a twenty-four-hour ordeal, as the steam engine of the train had malfunctioned, leaving them and all the passengers stranded.

With repairs complete and the train ready to depart, the trio took their seats.

"If this damn train hadn't broken down, Pritchard would be dead now," Ted complained.

Looking around nervously, Earl said, "Keep your voice down, cousin."

"I don't care what these people think," Ted spouted.

"That's the liquor talking," Earl said.

Fester had already curled up on his seat, his hat covering his eyes.

"I'll have you know, cousin, that it's not the liquor, it's just that I don't give a damn," Ted barked.

Lifting his hat off his face, Fester growled, "Ted, keep it down. I want to get some sleep." Fester had begun to grow weary of his youngest cousin, Ted. So much he was beginning to regret having sent him the telegram in the first place.

"That's all you do is sleep," Ted barked back.

"I know you're upset, Ted, but whether it's today or tomorrow, Randall Pritchard will be getting his," Earl said. "The thing we need to do is stick to our plan."

Ted laughed loudly.

"What's so funny?" Earl asked.

"The plan is to walk up and shoot the dumb bastard," Ted said.

Annoyed by Ted's bravado over the past two days, Fester sat up and asked, "Ted, how old are you?"

"What difference does it make?" Ted asked.

"You're not even eighteen," Fester reminded him.

"So what? Billy the Kid killed his first man when he was twelve or something. Age has nothing to do with it," Ted countered.

"All I'm saying is I know you've never killed a man much less shot at one. You can practice shooting bottles and tree knots all day, but when you square up against a man, it's different. So when Earl says we stick to the plan, we stick to the plan we made," Fester said in a chastising tone.

"Earl is only three years older than me, and I know he hasn't killed a man either," Ted protested.

"I know, but I also know that if we want to be successful, we need to have a plan and stick by it," Earl said.

The plan the men were discussing had been formulated earlier that day and started with them waiting until Randall parked himself in a gambling hall or saloon. They knew that taking him in his hotel room or boardinghouse would be stealthier, but they didn't just want to kill him, they wanted to send a message and wanted the world to know that the great Randall Pritchard was being killed for the murder of Randall Hoffman. After they located Pritchard, they'd each go in, one by one, and take up positions around Randall, being sure not to raise suspicions. Then Fester was chosen as the one who would approach Randall. He'd declare who he was, draw, and gun down Randall right where he sat. They all agreed that Fester should kill him because it was his brother they were avenging, but Ted had a burning desire to pull the trigger and deliver the fatal shot.

The train jerked ahead and slowly began to move. This resulted in the car erupting into a big cheer.

"Finally we're on our way," Ted grunted.

"Just get some sleep, and please, Ted, don't run your mouth too much," Fester said, leaning back and covering his eyes with his hat again.

"I can see why my pa left Michigan," Ted complained.

"Tickets, please. Tickets, please," the conductor shouted when he entered the car.

Earl held out the tickets for him and his cousins.

The conductor took them and tore them in half. "Here you go, sir."

"When will we arrive in Phoenix?" Earl asked.

"Tomorrow late morning. Get some shut-eye, and remember, we do have a food car two back," the conductor said as he proceeded to the next passengers.

Ted jumped up and said, "I'm going to go grab some grub. Anyone want to join me?"

Fester didn't reply.

"You go ahead," Earl said.

Ted strutted off.

"I know you're not asleep, so I'll tell you this, we need to keep an eye on Ted," Earl said.

Not lifting his head, Fester replied, "Don't worry, he's just excited is all. That'll all change once he's face-to-face with real danger. He won't do anything stupid. The one we need to worry about is Pritchard We all talk big, but he's a real threat. We need to make sure he goes down."

"You'll get him," Earl said.

Slightly lifting his hat, Fester said, "If I don't, take him; you hear me?"

"I hear you," Earl said.

"You'll be able to do that, won't you?" Fester asked.

"I will."

"You won't freeze, will ya?" Fester asked.

"Cousin, I won't freeze. You can trust me," Earl said.

"Good, now don't talk to me until we reach Phoenix," Fester said, lowering the hat and curling up.

Earl looked around. He was filled with excitement and dread. What was in store for them in Phoenix would be a defining moment in their lives if they survived.

***

Levi walked into the hotel and found the man he was looking for coming down the stairs.

"You again?" Randall roared. He was angry and ready for a fight.

Using every ounce of restraint and thinking of

142

Katherine, Levi walked up to Randall and said, "Mr. Pritchard, I'm here to see you."

"Are you here to continue where we left off earlier today?"

"No, I'm here to tell you that a man is planning to rob you tonight. I wanted you to know in the event my deputy and I aren't successful in finding him."

Randall cocked his head and asked, "Just this morning I think you wanted to kill me, and now you're here to warn me about a potential robbery?"

"I don't want to get into it, so take the warning and heed it," Levi said.

Clark was in the dining hall and spotted Levi and Randall talking. He raced out, his arms waving. "You two, don't do anything."

Randall raised his hand and said, "It's fine, Marshal. The sheriff came to warn me about a potential robbery."

"What's this?" Clark asked.

"I have a man in custody. He's sitting in my jail right now for the murder of Charlie Torrance and Brant Stone."

"I told you Brant Stone died accidentally," Clark fired back.

"Well, take that up with the man I have locked up. He admitted to the killing as well as implicated a man named Samuel. He even told me where I can find Samuel," Levi said.

"Are you just doing this to try to embarrass me?" Clark asked.

"No, Marshal, I have no interest in that, and as soon

as I'm done with this, I'm leaving Phoenix."

"Where are you going?" Clark asked.

"For a man who makes sure he's in the know, I'm shocked. I'm the next deputy United States marshal. I'll be working out of Prescott," Levi said.

"Congratulations," Clark said.

"You two carry on. I have a poker game to get to," Randall said and walked off.

"Mr. Pritchard, don't stay in your room tonight, not until I say it's okay to do so," Levi said.

Randall waved him off and said, "I've never met a man who could take me."

"I'll get him to move, don't you worry," Clark said.

"Any interest in joining me on this ride?" Levi asked.

"No, thank you, someone has to protect this town." Clark laughed. "And, Levi, good job. I swore Brant Stone died accidentally. I'm sure the widow Stone will be grateful to know the truth. In fact, I'll head over there and tell her," Clark said.

"How about I do that later?" Levi asked.

"Sure, you go ahead," Clark said, patting Levi on the shoulder. He turned and went back to the dining hall.

Levi went to leave, but a loud whistle caught his attention. He looked back and saw Randall signaling for him to come over. When he got to the table, Randall got up, pulled Levi aside, and said, "I'm glad we've patched things up."

Thinking only of Katherine, Levi stood and let Randall talk without emoting.

"And this Brant Stone, any relation to Savannah

Stone?" Randall asked.

"Her dead husband," Levi said.

"Damn, she won't like hearing that." Randall said what he was thinking.

"Do you know Mrs. Stone?" Levi asked.

For a split second, Randall thought about lying but decided he was done with that. Savannah already knew his identity. "She's my daughter."

Shocked by the news, Levi said, "My condolences for your son-in-law."

"It's fine, I didn't know him. In fact, I never met the lad, but heard he was a good man…well, up until recently," Randall said.

"I was going to go tell Mrs. Stone the news, but since she's your daughter, I expect you want to tell her," Levi said.

"No, that's not going to work. You see, my daughter doesn't care for me," Randall confessed.

Levi almost burst out in laughter. It appeared he wasn't alone in his dislike for Randall.

"You go ahead. I just wanted to confirm it was her husband. The poor thing has been through a lot. I wish she would receive my company. She's going to need a shoulder to cry on," Randall said.

"It's too bad you don't get along with her, nothing can be worse than a family squabble," Levi said, fully knowing what that felt like. It appeared he and Randall had something in common.

"Sheriff, I don't know what you had against me before, but like I said this morning, I pride myself on getting along with the law in each town I go to. I was disappointed we weren't seeing eye to eye, but now it appears we can have some sort of relationship. I don't expect us to be fast friends, but as long as we're not enemies, that's fine by me."

Levi could hear the wise words of Katherine ringing in his head. *Forgive…forgive.* That was something he couldn't quite do, but he would work on it, not for her but truly for himself.

"Have a good night, Sheriff, and I will switch rooms. I'd like to see tomorrow," Randall said and walked away.

Levi watched him until he sat down at his table. With only a few hours of light left, he now needed to get Thompson and head out to stop Samuel.

OUTSKIRTS OF PHOENIX, MARICOPA COUNTY, ARIZONA TERRITORY

The two rode hard until they reached the area Al told them they'd be able to find Samuel and the shack. With the terrain being difficult to travel, they ditched their horses and walked the remaining distance.

After hiking over boulders, they found the shack; it was about where Al said it was. A lone horse stood hitched outside, leading Levi to believe Samuel was still there and alone.

"Do you have those binoculars?" Levi asked.

"I sure do, Sheriff," Thompson said. He reached back and removed a set from a satchel and handed them over to Levi.

Levi placed them to his eyes. He focused them on an open window and spotted a man inside sitting at a table. "I think I see our man."

"Is he alone?" Thompson asked.

"Looks that way. Only one horse and I can only see one person. I think this might go easier than we thought," Levi said, lowering the binoculars. He handed them back to Thompson and said, "Shall we go arrest Samuel?"

Putting the binoculars back in the satchel, Thompson grinned and said, "That's what we do."

Levi came in from the left while Thompson swooped down from the right.

Levi reached the corner of the shack and waited for Thompson to appear.

Thompson came down, but before he could reach his corner, he tripped and fell face-first into the side of the shack with a loud thud.

Seeing Thompson's fall, Levi grimaced. He held his pistol in his grip, hammer back, and now felt he'd probably have to use it.

"Who the hell is out there? Is that your drunk ass, Al?" Samuel barked from inside.

Thompson got to his feet and gave Levi a sorrowful look.

Levi raised his finger over his lips, signaling for Thompson to remain quiet.

"Damn it, Al, where the hell have you been?" Samuel asked, throwing open the door and stepping out, a shotgun in his hands.

Knowing this was his opportunity, Levi came from

around the corner with the pistol leveled at Samuel. "I'm the sheriff. Put down the shotgun, Samuel."

Startled, Samuel jumped and began to turn towards Levi with the shotgun at his hip.

"Don't do it," Levi barked, seeing the muzzle of the shotgun coming towards him.

The crack of a gunshot sounded; it echoed off the surrounding rocks.

Samuel dropped the shotgun and looked bewildered as blood oozed from his mouth. A large red stain began to form on the front of his shirt.

Levi looked at his pistol. He hadn't fired, which could only mean Thompson had.

Samuel mumbled something unintelligible then crumpled to the ground, dead.

Cautiously walking towards the body, Levi said, "I suppose that takes care of this situation."

"Sorry, Sheriff, I know you wanted to arrest him, but when I saw him turning with that shotgun in your direction, I acted instinctually," Thompson said.

"It's quite alright, Deputy, quite all right," Levi said, kneeling down and checking to confirm Samuel was dead. "That was a clean shot."

"Thank you."

"No, thank you," Levi said, standing tall. He entered the shack to find a bag of cash and coin sitting on the table. "Look what we have here."

Thompson came in behind him and looked over his shoulder. "Do you suppose it belonged to Charlie Torrance?"

"Could be, and could also belong to Brant Stone," Levi said. Looking around the small twelve-by-ten-foot space, he said, "Tear apart the place and see if you can find anything else."

"Yes, Sheriff," Thompson said.

When they had finished searching the shack, they'd found another stash of cash and coin as well as several weapons. They took it all, strapped it and Samuel's body to his horse, and headed to get their horses.

"What should we do with the money?" Thompson said as they walked.

"Deputy, you're going to divide it up and give half to Mrs. Stone and the other half to any relative you can find of Charlie Torrance."

"You're not going to help me?" Thompson asked.

"Deputy, with this being over, I think I'm done being sheriff of Maricopa County. Time for you to take the reins."

"You're headed to Prescott early?" Thompson asked.

"I'm headed to Prescott, but first I need to go to Tucson."

"What's in Tucson?"

Placing his hand on Thompson's shoulder, Levi said, "I've got to get my family."

"I didn't know they were in Tucson. Odd, I just saw them this morning," Thompson said.

"It was a trip planned at the last minute," Levi said, deliberately keeping what had happened with Katherine to himself.

PHOENIX, ARIZONA TERRITORY

By the time Levi and Thompson dropped off Samuel's body to the undertaker and secured the monies in a safe in his office, it was too late to visit Mr. Deveron or Mrs. Stone; however, Levi did send Thompson to the Rising Sun Hotel to inform Randall that the threat against him was now over. He let Thompson go because he had been informed that the train to Tucson hadn't left, so that meant Katherine and Zeke were still in Phoenix. Burning with a desire to see them, he made for his house.

He climbed the wooden stairs, grabbed the knob and turned it, but found the door locked. He fumbled through his pocket until he found his keys. He inserted the key, turned it, unlocked the deadbolt, and opened the door, only to be greeted by darkness.

"Katherine, Zeke, are you here?" he asked, stepping across the threshold.

Nothing but silence.

He cried out again, "Katherine!"

Only his echo replied.

Distraught, he sauntered into the house, lit the first lantern he found, and went from room to room, only to find them empty. Making his way up to his bedroom, he found clothing strewn on the floor. He wasn't sure if it was from when he had hastily tried to pack them or from her. He sat on the edge of the bed. Never in his life had he made such a huge mistake. He had allowed unchecked emotions to rage in him to the point of almost losing everything he'd built and worked hard for. There was no doubt now that the rage that lived in his father was also in him, and that made him sick. He wouldn't allow what destroyed his father and ultimately killed his mother to do the same to him and his family. No, he would stop and stop now. He would make amends, and the first place to go was the Rising Sun Hotel.

With renewed purpose, he got up and raced out of the house.

***

Levi strutted into the Rising Sun Hotel, past the front desk, and directly into the dining hall. He looked around but didn't see Randall or any tables set up to play poker. He went back to the front desk and asked, "No poker tonight?"

"No, Sheriff, not tonight, and if you're looking for Mr. Pritchard, I heard he's playing down the street at the Desert Rose," Dale said.

"Thank you," Levi said and promptly left. He rushed down to the Desert Rose, walked in, and was instantly greeted by a cloud of cigar and pipe smoke and the aroma of stale beer. A raucous crowd was near the back of the packed bar. He pushed his way past the patrons until he was next to the table where Randall was playing.

Randall gave him a quick glance and said, "Your deputy informed me, thank you."

"Is that why you're playing here tonight?" Levi asked.

"I'll raise you fifteen," Randall said, tossing a few coins into the center of the table. He shot Levi another look and said, "That's exactly why; thought I'd play it safe. I don't want to end up like Wild Bill in Deadwood."

"When you're done with your game, I need to talk to you. It's very important," Levi said.

"I can tell by the look on your face it's urgent. Just give me a moment," Randall said.

"Hey, Sheriff, I've got a drink here at the bar, on the house for what you did earlier today with Dirty Al," the bartender announced.

Levi craned his head back and saw the bartender waving him over. Levi went to the bar, but it was packed, not an inch to squeeze in.

"You two, move the hell over. The sheriff is here to get his drink," the bartender barked at the men in front of Levi.

They both gave Levi a scowl then moved out of his way.

Levi took the shot glass of whiskey, raised it, and said, "Thank you."

"No, thank you, that dirty son of a bitch was always in here stinking up the place," the bartender said.

"Dirty Al, I didn't know that was his name," Levi said, tossing the shot back.

"Not sure if it's his name or a description," the bartender joked.

"He did kinda smell." Levi laughed.

Randall tapped Levi on the shoulder and asked, "You wanted to talk?"

Sliding the glass back to the bartender, Levi said, "Thank you again."

"No, Sheriff, thank you, and I owe you a few more. Have a good night," the bartender said, giving Levi a nod.

Levi led Randall outside so he could talk privately and without having to raise his voice.

Out front, Randall pulled a pipe from his pocket, packed the bowl, and lit it. The sweet-smelling smoke rose, hitting Levi's nostrils.

"I never took up smoking," Levi said.

"It's probably what caused my damn cancer," Randall said then took a few puffs.

"You have cancer?" Levi asked, shocked to hear the news.

"That's why I'm here. I'm dying. Hell, I'll probably be in the ground within the month at the rate it feels like its spreading. Each morning it's getting harder and harder to rise, and I'm now coughing up fleshy stuff and lots of blood. Trust me, Sheriff, you don't want cancer," Randall said.

"I wasn't aware you were sick," Levi said, now feeling even more foolish that he almost ruined his life murdering a man who would be dead within a month anyway.

"So what do you have to talk about?" Randall asked.

Levi sighed loudly.

"This is going to be good. I can tell by the sigh," Randall jested.

"I met you a long time ago, back in Wichita. I was ten years old."

"We've met before? Hmm, I'm sure it wasn't playing poker, being that you were ten," Randall said as he ground his teeth on the pipe stem.

"I wasn't playing poker; you played my father. He challenged you, and like you always do, you won, but this time your winnings were every cent my family had. You see, my father was a drunk, a tough man who took his anger out on me and my ma. I guess you could say he wasn't a good father, but he was what God gave me. I pleaded with you that night not to play him. I implored you to just let him leave, but you didn't; in fact, you taunted him. My father then sat down, and in one hand you took every penny we had."

"Wait, I remember you. Yes, you were the persistent lad. I seem to recall your father struck you that night."

"He did."

"I also recall I told him I wasn't going to play him."

"I don't recall that. No, you taunted my father," Levi said, challenging Randall's recollection.

"Sheriff, I remember that night vividly. What you didn't see because you weren't there is me offering your father several opportunities to back away. He got angry, even struck the table with his fist. Now when I see a man so passionate about wanting to play and I've given them all the exits, but they keep insisting, I play. When you arrived, I again offered him an out, maybe twice; yet he hit you and still insisted on playing."

Levi wanted to argue, but let Randall's words simmer and marinate in his mind.

"So you've been angry with me all these years because your father lost a game of poker against me?" Randall asked.

"No, Mr. Pritchard, I'm angry because of what he did

after that."

Taking a puff on his pipe, Randall asked, "And that was?"

"He went home in a fit of rage, killed my mother, shot me, and put the pistol to his head and blew his brains out."

Randall's mouth hung open. He was shocked by the revelation.

"For all these years I've held you responsible for him killing my mother. His loss to you sent him over the edge."

"And now suddenly you don't think I'm responsible?" Randall asked.

"I'm struggling with that, have been since I heard you'd arrived in town. My wife thinks you're innocent, and I, well, I'm coming around to that," Levi said, biting his lip as he talked.

"I'm so very sorry about what happened to your dear mother and yourself. How horrific," Randall said sincerely.

"Mr. Pritchard, I came here to tell you that I've forgiven you for that night. Whatever your part was in it, I absolve you," Levi said. He could feel a sense of calm wash over him.

"That must have been difficult for you to say," Randall said, now thinking of Jane.

"The idea was difficult, but now that it's done, it feels good. I feel liberated," Levi said.

"Good."

"And please accept my apologies for how I treated you before," Levi said, sticking his hand out.

Randall looked at it with a raised brow and said, "You have turned the other cheek." He took Levi's hand and shook. "If you're done, I need to get going. I have some things I need to attend to."

"Get back to your game," Levi said.

"No, I'm done with that for tonight. You've inspired me, Sheriff. I'm going to go see someone and do what you've so proudly done…forgive them," Randall said. "Have a good night, Sheriff."

"You too."

Stopping a few feet away, Randall turned and said, "Thank you, Sheriff, and I mean it, thank you."

Not knowing how to respond, Levi simply said, "Good night, Mr. Pritchard."

***

Inspired by Levi's confession and contriteness, Randall rushed to the hotel as fast as his heaving chest would allow. He whisked himself up the stairs and down the narrow hall, stopping in front of Jane's door. He reached up to knock but paused. Unsure what time it was, he pulled his pocket watch out of his vest and opened it to reveal the time was close to ten. Was it too late? Should he wake her for this?

As he debated what to do outside, inside Jane had been lying on the bed, unable to sleep. She heard the footfalls coming and stopping at her door. A strong inclination told her who it was. She tossed the covers off, went to the door, and opened it wide.

Surprised, Randall said, "I was meaning to knock; then I saw what time—"

Before he could finish, she grabbed him by the arm

and pulled him inside the room, slamming the door behind him. "I'm happy you came."

"Jane, I want to apologize," he blurted out. Just using the word *sorry* or *apologize* was unfamiliar in his lexicon.

"No, no, I'm the one who is sorry; I interfered, and like I said earlier, I will fix it. I've been thinking—"

Now cutting her off, Randall placed a couple of fingers over her lips and said, "Ssh, please let me finish what I was saying."

She smiled and nodded.

"Tonight something happened that I never thought I'd see. Remember how I told you about the sheriff and how he'd treated me?"

She nodded.

"He came to see me not minutes ago and told me an interesting story. He told me that the reason he had acted the way he did was because he hated me and in the most vicious of ways. You see, I had met him before, many years ago when he was a child not older than ten. I played poker with his father and beat him badly, taking the family's last dollar. The sheriff, Levi is his name, pleaded with me then to not play his father, but I did, and to defend myself, I gave his father many chances to walk away," Randall said then cleared his throat. "We played and I beat him. Well, Levi's father didn't take kindly to that. He went home that night, got his pistol, and killed Levi's mother, shot Levi, then turned it on himself."

Covering her mouth in horror, Jane gasped. "Oh my."

"It's tragic, truly," Randall said. "Well, tonight, he came and told me that he'd forgiven me for what he perceived as a transgression. You see, he blamed me for what happened that night. He held me responsible for the death of his mother and father."

"But you didn't do anything. It was all his father," Jane said.

"Correct, but to a young boy, all he could remember was me being there. He didn't know that I'd given his father many chances to walk away. He didn't seem to recall I even gave him another out when Levi stood there. All he remembered after all those years was me beating his father and taking their last few dollars."

"And now it's all forgiven?" Jane asked.

"Yes, just like that. How a man can harbor such feelings for so long only to let them go is powerful."

"It seems to me he had a reason, no doubt one that outweighed the other," Jane said.

"What he did got me thinking. I've only known you for a short time, but I can just feel that our time together was meant to happen. This isn't an accident. And I also know that you would never try to harm me whatsoever," he said. Reaching out and touching the top of her chest, he continued. "You have a big heart, you're a sweet and wise woman, and I don't want to live my last few days or weeks without you. So will you please forgive me for acting like a damn old fool?"

"There's nothing to forgive," she said, her eyes filling with tears.

"There's much to forgive. Can we start new, fresh?"

"Of course," she said.

The two embraced.

"Will you stay with me tonight?" she asked.

He nodded.

Taking his hand, she led him to her bed.

CHAPTER SEVEN

JUNE 16, 1896

PHOENIX, ARIZONA TERRITORY

Levi woke feeling like he had accomplished much to move him in the direction of being back in Katherine's good graces; however, he wasn't done just yet. He still had a few more things to do before he could officially relinquish his duties as sheriff.

He rose the second the sun did, got cleaned up, dressed, and was out the door in minutes. His first stop would be Mrs. Stone's house after a quick stop at the office to pick up the monies he presumed were her dead husband's

As he approached the house, he spotted a man leaving. Drawing closer, he saw it was Mr. Sullivan, the bank manager. "Good day, Mr. Sullivan."

"Oh, hello there, Sheriff. Here to see the widow Stone?" he asked, climbing onto his wagon.

"I am. I pray what I'm about to tell her is good news to her ears," Levi said.

"It seems like she's having one heck of a day so far," Sullivan said, reaching forward to take the reins.

"You came bearing gifts too?" Levi asked, climbing off his horse.

"I'd say so. I thought it was appropriate considering her situation to deliver to her the title of her land that she now has back. An anonymous donor paid off her mortgage."

Shocked by the news, Levi said, "That is a nice gift."

Tipping his hat, Sullivan said, "Have a good day, Sheriff."

Levi waved. He went to the door, but before he could knock, Savannah opened it.

"Morning, Sheriff," she said.

"Mrs. Stone, I hope my visit is timely," Levi said politely.

"Please, come on in," she said, opening the door wide.

Over his shoulder, Levi carried a heavy canvas sack. He walked in and set it on the table with a thud.

"What is that?" she asked.

"Before I answer that, I want to tell you that it was confirmed. Your husband was murdered." Levi went on to detail everything Al had told him.

Savannah took a seat and sighed. Even though Levi had told her before that he suspected it, to finally have it confirmed filled her with sorrow. "My poor husband."

"I am sorry for your loss," Levi said. "Now let's discuss what's in the sack."

"It's money, isn't it?" she asked.

"It is. It's half of the money we found. We don't know

of anyone else who was ensnared in their plot, so we divided it between you, and the other half will find its way to a relative of Charlie Torrance."

"How much?"

"Three thousand two hundred and seventeen dollars," Levi said, turning the sack over and emptying the contents onto the table.

Savannah watched in amazement as the cash and coins poured out.

"I should also tell you that your husband won that night he gambled," Levi said. "I know that's not really a consolation prize, but I thought you should know."

"I'd rather have him back," Savannah said.

"Mrs. Stone, if I'm prying, please let me know, but can I offer a bit of advice?" Levi asked.

"Sure."

"Sell this house and land, and move back to where you came from, where family is," he said, presuming she had family.

Savannah folded her hands and frowned. "Today is proving to be an interesting day. Mr. Sullivan just informed me that someone paid off my mortgage."

"That's a nice gift," Levi said.

"It was my father; he did it," she guessed, although Mr. Sullivan never told her who the donor was.

"You're father did that for you?"," Levi asked, fully knowing who her father was but not sure if he should open up about that knowledge.,.

"My father is in Phoenix, but I don't have any interest in seeing him," she confessed.

"Sorry to hear that. Do you have other family? Your mother?"

"She's dead."

"Family means everything to me. It's why I went and did something I never thought I'd do," Levi said. He looked at an empty chair and asked, "Mind if I sit?"

"Please, and can I offer you something to drink?" she asked.

"I'm fine, thank you," he said. "I don't know you, but I want to share a story with you. Maybe it will help." Levi told her about Randall, his father, what had happened those many years ago, and then what he did last night and why.

Savannah sat not saying a word, her mouth hanging open in shock.

"I forgave him, and I have to tell you, I feel good about it. Now I'm here finishing up some responsibilities; then I'm headed to Tucson to get my family."

"He's my father," Savannah blurted out suddenly.

" Mrs. Stone, I need to confess something to you for I feel awkward," Levi said.

"What's that, sheriff?" she asked.

"I already knew Randall Pritchard was your father, he confided in me last night after he and I
spoke," Levi said.

"Then did he put you up to this, the money, all of this?" she asked suspicious.

"No, he didn't," Levi said.

"Hearing what you went through at his hands, I don't see how you forgave him," Savannah said.

"I never thought I could do it either, but after doing so, I feel liberated," Levi said. "I only say this as a suggestion so please don't be upset, but I think you should also consider forgiving him. I know what happened to you as a child and I know he wasn't a model father but the second you let go of that anger you'll feel better."

"Thank you for the advice, sheriff but I don't think I can ever find it in me," Savannah said.

"None of this is a coincidence, I feel there might be a higher power at play here," Levi said.

"You think this is God's work?" Savannah asked.

"It must be," Levi said.

"My father abandoned me and my mother when I was a child. I never heard from him until years later when I received a letter. I promptly replied telling him to leave me alone; then he shows up at the general store pretending to be someone else."

"You didn't know what he looked like?" Levi asked.

"No."

"So he went to the store and was pretending to be someone else?"

"Yes."

"He wanted to see you; that's what he was doing," Levi said, feeling sympathetic to Randall's cause.

"He lied again is what that was. Then he sent some woman. She stands in the store proclaiming that he's a good man, flawed yet still good. That he didn't abandon us, that he had been told to leave by my mother, and he left when I was three years old. That too is a lie. My mother told me he left us when I was an infant."

"Why don't you give him a chance?"

"He had his chance when I was a child and he didn't care," Savannah said.

"I shouldn't be saying this, but you should know he's dying," Levi said.

Savannah furrowed her brow and thought. "That woman mentioned something about him dying. I thought it had to do with him wanting to see me before he died, like see me again, not that he knew he was actually dying."

"He's got cancer, and just last night he told me he may not make it until the end of the month," Levi said.

She stewed on what he said, letting it sink in. However, after much thought, she still couldn't find the same ability to forgive that Levi did. "I can't do it. I won't. If he wanted to see me or be a part of my life, he could have done so years ago."

Levi nodded. He didn't want to pry or apply pressure. "Fair enough."

"Sheriff, unless there's something else, I need to get to the store and open it up," Savannah said.

He looked at the pile of money and asked, "You're still going to go to work?"

Standing tall, she replied, "I gave my word to Mr. Montgomery that I'd help him, and I will continue to do so until he doesn't need me anymore."

Levi stood, took his hat, and headed to the door. He opened it and walked out. Turning back around, he said, "Take care, Mrs. Stone."

"Goodbye, Sheriff."

***

Jane woke to find Randall wasn't in her room. She touched the side of the bed he'd been sleeping on and wished he was still there. Having him stay over had made her feel whole again.

The door of her room opened suddenly, and in came Randall wearing only a robe. "Oh, good, you're awake," he said. In his hands was a cigar box. He scurried over to the bed and sat down next to Jane. "I had an idea this morning when I woke. In this box is every letter I sent Savannah as she was growing up. As you can see on the envelope, they're all return to sender. Now some got back to me while others didn't." Handing her one of the letters, he continued, "As you can see, it's not open. They're all like that."

"She never let Savannah read them," Jane said. She picked up more letters and fingered through them. "Not one was opened. The woman didn't let her read them. I know where you're going with this."

"I'm going to take them over to her this morning. I know she'll refuse, but I'll leave them with her. If she decides to read them, then she'll see the man I am…at least that's what I hope. There's also the letter her mother wrote me asking me to leave. It's all in there as well as this," he said, taking a tin photograph out and handing it to Jane.

Jane looked at the photograph of a much younger Randall, a woman she presumed was his then wife, and Savannah, who at the time must have been two years old. "A once happy family," she said, gently touching the faces in the picture.

"This will prove I was with them after she was born," he said.

"This is a good idea. Can I do anything to help?" Jane asked, caressing his arm.

"Just pray."

"I will."

Excited about the possibility, Randall jumped out of bed and began to get dressed.

"You're leaving now?" Jane asked.

"Yes, how about when I return, we meet up for a late breakfast or maybe tea?" he said, buttoning his shirt.

Curling up on the bed, she replied, "Sounds wonderful."

Randall finished getting his clothes on, grabbed the box, and just before he went to the door, he gave Jane a kiss on the lips. "I'll see you in a bit."

"Good luck," she said.

"Thank you," he said then raced out the door.

***

Fester stepped off the train and took in a deep breath. "What is that smell?" he asked as Earl stepped up next to him.

"What smell?" Earl asked.

"The air, it smells nothing like Michigan," Fester replied.

Coming up behind them, Ted howled, "The only thing I smell is that bastard shitting his pants once he sees us."

"Stick to the plan," Earl warned Ted.

"Cousin, stop saying that. I didn't travel all the way to Arizona Territory to foul up what we're here to do," Ted assured him.

"Good," Earl said. "Now what, Fester?"

"I think I could move out here. It's beautiful in its own way. I don't miss the green," Fester said, looking back towards the flat open desert and the mountains beyond. He removed his hat and waved it against his face. "What time is it? It's getting warm."

"Welcome to Arizona," Earl said. "I heard it gets hot as hades here."

"How hot?" Ted asked.

"Over a hundred on many days in the summer," Earl said. "A man once told me that it got to one hundred and twenty degrees here."

"Damn, that's hot," Ted exclaimed.

"I sorta like it," Fester said, his eyes pressed closed as he took in another deep breath.

"You really thinkin' of moving out here?" Ted asked.

"Yeah, I really like it," Fester said.

"What on earth will you do?" Ted asked.

"I don't know. I suppose they need laborers for any number of things," Fester said. "Heck, I bet I could go get a job today if I needed one. I heard a man on the train talking about working in orange orchards around here."

"You working picking oranges would be something to see." Ted laughed.

"What the hell is so funny about that? I'm thinking

about doing that," Fester countered.

"What will your parents say about you coming out here?" Earl asked.

"Don't matter to me what they say. I'm my own man. I only wish I could have seen this before. I could've gotten Ronald to come with me, keep him out of trouble," Fester said, his tone turning melancholy.

"Well, if you move out here, make sure you visit me more. You'll only be a day's train travel from me," Earl said.

Several men walked by; one gave Ted a quizzical stare.

"What the hell you looking at?" Ted barked at the man.

Stunned by Ted's aggressive response, the man turned his head away and sheepishly moved on along with his colleagues.

"Did you see that?" Ted asked.

"Don't make a scene. We're here to do one thing and one thing only. We don't need the attention," Fester said.

"Can we go now?" Ted asked.

"Yeah, let's go find Pritchard and avenge my brother," Fester said.

***

Randall paused several times before entering the general store. There he found Mr. Montgomery standing at the counter, with two customers looking around.

Seeing him, Montgomery let out an audible sigh and

hollered, "Mrs. Stone, can you come here?"

"Sure thing, Mr. Montgomery," Savannah said from the storeroom. She came out the door, her head down as she tied her apron. Looking up, she saw Randall. "No. You need to go."

Humbly walking towards her, Randall held out the cigar box and said, "Please just take these, please."

"No," she said, one hand on her hip, the other pointing to the door.

He took several steps closer and repeated what he said before.

"What is it?" she asked.

"The letters. Letters I wrote you over the years, but your mother returned unopened. If you read them, you'll get an idea of how much I missed you and—"

"Leave them and go," she said.

"Can I say something more?" he asked.

The couple of shoppers in the store stood and watched the back-and-forth, causing Montgomery to grow impatient. "Can you two take this outside?"

Savannah stood rigid, her nostrils flaring, "Fine, and I'm only giving you a minute, nothing more."

"Thank you," Randall said. He hurried to the door, opened it, and stepped aside. "After you."

Savannah smirked and said, "You're such a gentleman."

Closing the door behind him, Randall walked up to her and said, "In that box you'll also find the letter your mother wrote me demanding I leave. It was her, not me, who made that decision. She didn't like that I gambled…wait, she liked it until the day you were born; then she protested. After a few tense years, she wrote me the letter you'll find in that box, and left it for me. She didn't even give me the courtesy of seeing you one more time. She took what money we had and took off with you. It took me months, but I found you, and again she wouldn't allow me to see you. It was then that I began to question if maybe my life was one not conducive to be a proper father. I did write you though, but in that box you'll see they were all returned unopened. She never allowed you to see them much less read them. I heard that she told you I abandoned you at childbirth; that's not true. We all lived under the same roof for three years. It's sad to know you don't remember any of those memories. All I wanted to do was to say I was sorry, sorry that I didn't fight harder to be with you, sorry that it didn't work out, sorry that you didn't have a father as you grew up, sorry that I was too pigheaded and selfish not to stop gambling so I could be with you. The truth is, while I didn't abandon you like she described, I did let you go, and for that I'm deeply sorry. I don't expect you to forgive me, and I want nothing from you except to hear from me. I love you, Savannah, and I'm so proud of the woman you've become."

She fought it, but tears began to streak down her face.

He took out a handkerchief and held it out for her.

At first she refused to take it, but the tears began to really flow, forcing her to snatch it from his hand. She dabbed her cheeks and eyes. "Is that all?"

"I had a will and testament drafted. It's with a local attorney in town, a man by the name of Gibbs. When I die, please go see him."

"The sheriff told me this morning you're dying. Is that true?" she asked, sniffling.

"It is. I have cancer. The doctor in Dodge City said I could go by next week or in two months, but either way the cancer will kill me," he confirmed.

"You come to finally see me and you're dying. How do you think that makes me feel?" Savannah said as more tears flowed.

He stepped towards her.

She in turn walked back from his advance. "Don't."

"I can't give you an adequate answer for my behavior. Just know that you were always in my thoughts. If I can at least give you the comfort of having my fortune, will you accept?"

"You think I want your money?" she asked.

"No, I know you don't, but will you take it?" he asked.

"Maybe I'll take it then give it all away," she sniped.

"Do with it what you want. I won't need it where I'm going," he quipped.

"It was you who paid off my mortgage, wasn't it?" she asked.

"Yes."

"I suppose I owe you a bit of gratitude," she said.

"I'm glad I could do it, and I'm sorry about your husband. The sheriff told me what really happened to him," Randall said.

"Life hasn't been kind to me. I don't know why, but that's been my life," she lamented. Looking through the window, she saw Montgomery staring out at her. "I have to go back to work."

"Thank you for allowing me to explain, and if you want, please read those letters."

"I'll think about it," she said. Her thoughts then went to Jane. "Who was that woman in here?"

"She's a dear friend."

"Poor thing was in here selling her jewelry," Savannah revealed.

"Selling her jewelry?" Randall asked, shocked to hear it.

"Yes, she said she was on hard times like I was just recently. She sold five items to Mr. Montgomery for thirteen dollars."

"Is the jewelry still here?" he asked.

"As far as I know," Savannah said.

The two walked back inside and headed for the counter.

Montgomery was at the counter still, now receiving payment from the customers.

Savannah went behind the counter, unlocked the glass cabinet, and pulled out Jane's jewelry. "This is what she sold."

Randall gave Montgomery a look and asked, "How much for all of this?"

"Twenty-five dollars," he replied.

The two customers finished their sale and left, allowing Montgomery to give his full attention to the sale of the jewelry.

"But you bought it for thirteen," Savannah bellowed, shocked by his price increase.

"That's called business, my dear," Montgomery growled.

"Doesn't matter," Randall said, removing his wallet and fishing out the exact amount. "Can you box them up for me?"

Savannah packaged the jewelry and handed it to Randall.

"One last thing. I don't hold anything against your mother. She did what she felt was best. All in all, we both made some mistakes, and you were the one who was the victim of it all."

Montgomery loudly cleared his throat, signaling he was growing impatient with Savannah not working.

"I really do need to go," she said.

"Can we talk later?" he asked.

"I don't know. Let me think about it," she said.

"Fair enough," he said then turned and exited the store.

"I need to finish the inventory," Savannah said quickly before grabbing the cigar box and heading into the storeroom, closing the door behind her.

***

After asking around, Fester, Earl and Ted finally found someone who knew who Randall was and where he might be. The trio made their way to the Desert Rose bar first, then were told he could be found at the Rising Sun Hotel. Upon entering, they found a few people milling about in the lobby with a half dozen folks in the dining hall adjacent.

Fester went directly to the front desk and asked, "Have you seen Randall Pritchard?"

"He just left about ten minutes ago. I expect he'll be back shortly. Do you wish to leave him a message?" Dale asked.

"No," Fester said, Ted and Earl flanking him.

Dale gave the men a once-over and could suddenly sense something was off about them.

"Can we get food in there?" Ted asked, pointing to the dining hall.

"Yes, sir," Dale replied.

"C'mon, let's grab some grub," Ted said, sauntering off.

Fester tipped his hat and followed Ted to the dining hall, with Earl close behind.

The trio found a table, sat, and waited.

A waiter spotted them, walked up, and asked, "Can I help you, gentlemen?"

"A whiskey," Ted said.

"No whiskey, we'll take some breakfast. Bring us all two eggs each with bacon," Fester said.

"Why can't I have whiskey?" Ted groaned.

The waiter stood staring in case the order changed.

Glaring at him, Fester said, "Run off now and get us the food. Pay no mind to him."

The waiter rushed off.

Fester put his attention back on Ted and said, "We're here to get revenge for my brother. Until that's done, we're not drinking. We're staying focused, do you understand me?"

"But—"

"Ted, I'm not sure what's gotten into you. You seemed like you were up to the task, but lately you're acting like you may not be," Fester said, scolding him.

"I can drink—"

Again cutting him off, Fester's patience had run out. He reached across the table and slapped Ted in the face. "Listen up, cousin. Stop the bull."

"You hit me!" Ted exclaimed.

"Set yourself straight. Any minute he could walk in here. I need you focused. If all you want to do is drink, then leave, go back to that bar," Fester snapped.

"Fester is right, cousin," Earl said.

Biting his tongue, Ted looked away and sat simmering in his anger.

Fester leaned across the table again, but this time he only asked a question. "Do we have an understanding?"

"Yes," Ted said under his breath.

"I can't hear you," Fester growled.

"YES," Ted said, raising his voice.

"Good, now sit there, keep your mouth shut, and when your food comes, eat it. If Pritchard walks in that door, follow my lead," Fester ordered.

"Okay."

"Are we good, Earl?" Fester asked.

"I'm good," Earl replied.

"I'm glad we all see eye to eye. When we're done, we can all go celebrate over a bottle of whiskey," Fester said.

***

Dale kept his eye on the three and felt something was off about them. Going with his gut instinct, he called a valet over.

The valet, a young man named John, rushed over. "Yes."

"I need you to run over to the marshal's office. Tell whoever is there that we might be having some trouble here," Dale said.

"Trouble? Like what kind?" John asked, the expression on his face turning to concern.

"See those three men sitting at the far wall?" Dale asked.

John slowly turned his head, spotted Fester and his cousins, and replied, "The three dingy-looking fellas on the far wall underneath the painting of the saguaro?"

"Yes, that's them. They came in asking for Mr. Pritchard, but something tells me they're a bit off," Dale said.

"You think they're here to kill him?" John asked.

"I don't know, but out of an abundance of caution, let's get the marshal over here to talk to them," Dale said.

"Okay, I'll go now," John said and raced out of the hotel entrance. He sprinted across the street and down half a block to Marshal Clark's office. He burst through the door and hollered, "Where's Marshal Clark?"

Clark, who had been asleep at his desk, jumped up, startled. "What's going on?"

John ran up to his desk and said, "Marshal, there's

some men at the Rising Sun; I think they might mean to harm Mr. Pritchard."

"What do you mean?" Clark asked, rubbing his eyes.

"I mean they might be there to gun him down," John said. "Come, hurry."

Clark hopped to his feet, grabbed his hat from the table, and scurried out the door.

***

Savannah put the last letter down and picked up a handkerchief to wipe the tears that were streaming down her cheeks. In the bottom of the box sat the tin photograph. She picked it up and looked at the smiling faces emblazoned on it.

She recognized Randall and of course her mother, but could only assume the child was her. Was Randall telling the truth? She'd read the letter from her mother to him, and now she was looking at a photograph that clearly showed him and her mother and a child who had to be her. Why would her mother lie? she asked herself. Why did she not allow her to read his letters? What had he done that was so bad that she wanted to cut her off from him? Was he truly a bad man? Or was she just not in love with him anymore?

Confused by her entire family history, including her childhood and the stories she had been told by her mother, she decided she needed to talk to Randall more. Only he could piece together these missing parts and help her have a better understanding of what had happened and why.

She pushed the box aside, got to her feet, and marched out of the storeroom. Brushing past Montgomery, she said, "I'm taking a break. I'll be back shortly."

"You're leaving? But I need you—"

"I need to take a break. I'll do whatever you need when I return," she said, not flinching or stopping on her way out the door.

"I need you now," Montgomery said.

She stopped and said, "If you're not going to give me a break, then I need to take my leave of this employment."

"But, no, wait," Montgomery said.

Savannah flung open the door and headed out.

**

Clark ran into Levi as he marched down the street towards the Rising Sun.

"Sheriff, I need your help. My deputies aren't in, and there might be some trouble," Clark said.

"What sort of trouble?" Levi asked.

"The valet here said there's some men at the hotel, and they might be there to do some harm to Mr. Pritchard."

"Then let's go talk to these gentlemen," Levi said, finding the irony that once again he was going to the aid of the man whom just a day ago he had wanted to kill himself.

Ready to do what was needed, Clark and Levi headed in the direction of the hotel.

**

On his way back to the hotel, Randall made a stop at a street vendor who sold flowers. He purchased a bouquet of *Gerbera* daisies to give to Jane as a present for helping him with Savannah.

He stepped up on the walkway and headed into the hotel.

As he passed the front desk, Dale called out, "Mr. Pritchard?"

Randall stopped. "Good evening, Dale. What is it?"

"Sir, those gentlemen over there, the three seated in the dining hall underneath the painting of the saguaro, are looking for you. It's best I tell you that something seems off about them," Dale said.

Randall turned and looked, only to lock eyes with Fester.

"That's him," Fester said.

"Where?" Earl asked, his back facing Randall.

Ted craned his head to the right and said, "That's gotta be the son of a bitch."

Randall's experience and intuition told him Dale was right. The men now staring at him weren't there to chat; they'd come looking for a fight. "Thank you, Dale. I suggest you go find somewhere else to be."

"I sent word to the marshal," Dale said.

Not taking his eyes off Fester and his cousins, Randall said, "Why, thank you, Dale, you're a good man. Remind me to tip you later."

"Yes, sir," Dale said, not flinching and holding to his spot.

Randall handed him the bouquet and the package and said, "Take this up to Mrs. Tyne, would you?"

Taking the bouquet and package, Dale said, "Yes, sir."

Never one to back down, Randall cracked his neck and said, "Let's go see what these gentlemen want."

"Sir, don't go over there," Dale urged.

"Dale, just deliver those flowers for me. This I've got," Randall said then headed towards Fester and his cousins.

"He's coming this way. Hold tight, boys," Fester said, taking his right hand off the table and placing it on his lap.

Ted wasn't as subtle. He pulled his right hand back quickly, placing his open palm on the back strap of his pistol.

For Earl, his position was untenable due to his back facing the lobby. "He's coming?"

"Sit tight, everyone. Soon this will be over," Fester said.

Randall entered the dining hall, stopping six feet from the table. "Are you looking for me?"

Fester grinned and asked, "Are you Randall Pritchard?"

"Depends on who's looking?" Randall quipped, his right arm hanging long and straight against his side. He was known for his quick draw and shooting on the move, something few average gunfighters could do.

"My name is Fester. These are my cousins, Ted and Earl."

"Fester, Ted, Earl, what business do you have with Randall Pritchard?"

"Are you him, huh?" Ted spat.

"Like I said, depends on who's asking," Randall said, being cryptic.

"Are you him or not? It's a simple question," Ted shot back.

A large grin stretched across Randall's face. He could see the fear and anxiety in Ted's face. He'd seen men like him, young, dumb and cocky.

"If I was, how could I help you?" Randall asked.

The intensity in the room could be felt. The other patrons of the dining hall got up from their tables and scurried away.

"You boys are scaring away the customers," Randall joked.

Fester's right hand slowly made its way to his right hip.

Sizing everyone up, Randall now believed he could take them. His plan was to shoot Fester first because he seemed like the older, more calm and experienced fighter. Ted would be second, only because his hand was on his pistol and he'd draw quicker than Earl, who would go down without even being able to turn around.

"What do you want with Mr. Pritchard?" Randall asked.

"We need to talk to him. Are you him?" Fester asked again, trying to get Randall to confirm his identity.

The front door of the hotel opened and in came Savannah. She entered the lobby, went to the front desk, and asked Dale, who was hiding near the corner of the room. "Where's Mr. Pritchard?"

Dale pointed.

Asking loudly, she said, "Where?"

Hearing Savannah's voice sent a shiver down Randall's spine. She was in the hotel and now possibly in harm's way. He had to act now if he were to keep her safe.

Unable to control himself, Ted drew first. "Die, you son of a bitch!" he screamed as he stood and pulled his pistol from his holster.

Randall broke leather, cocked the pistol with his left palm, and squeezed off a round from the hip. The .45-caliber round exploded out of the muzzle, striking Ted in the stomach.

Savannah cried out when the first shot rang out.

Randall pivoted towards Fester, but he was too late. Fester had drawn while seated, cocked, and pulled the trigger. The bullet hit Randall in the upper torso, just below the right clavicle.

Randall lost his grip on his pistol and dropped it.

Hearing the gunshots from outside, Levi and Clark took off in a hard sprint towards the hotel.

Seeing his opportunity, Fester got to his feet, cocked his pistol again, raised it, took center aim at Randall, and pulled the trigger again. This shot struck Randall squarely in the chest. He recoiled and fell down, smacking his head on the hardwood floor.

Savannah cried out upon seeing Randall fall. Running on nothing but instinct, she ran towards him. "No."

After decades of gunfights, Randall was done and with a potentially fatal wound. He coughed and blood spewed out.

Fester cocked the pistol again and marched towards

Randall, who lay crawling on the floor. Stopping just above him, Fester looked down and said, "You killed my brother. Prepare to die."

"No," Savannah screamed.

Fester looked up and saw her coming at him. He raised his pistol and began to apply pressure to the trigger.

Still able to make sense of what was happening, Randall reached out and grabbed Fester by the leg and forced him down.

Fester toppled over.

Another gunshot rang out; this time it was Earl. He'd finally gotten up, drawn, and had fired a single shot, hitting Randall in the hip.

Randall cried out in pain.

Savannah reached Randall and laid her body upon his. "Don't shoot him!" she screamed.

Getting to his feet, Fester barked, "I'll shoot you down too, woman."

"Leave him be," Savannah cried out.

"I don't have time for this," Fester said.

"You can't shoot a woman," Earl protested.

A gunshot cracked. This time it came from Levi's pistol. As usual his aim was true. The bullet struck Fester in the side of the head.

Fester dropped straight down to the ground and fell onto his side, dead.

Fearing for his life now, Earl turned and ran towards the door that led to the kitchen.

Levi took two steps forward, cocked his pistol again, aimed, and let another round loose.

The bullet punched through the center of Earl's back and out his chest. He crashed forward, landing on a table and crashing onto the floor.

Cocking again, Levi advanced into the dining room. He went to Earl, saw him move, and fired another shot, this time killing him.

Ted groaned to Levi's left, blood pouring from his mouth and tears streaming down his face. "I don't wanna die," he sobbed. He coughed a few times then took his last breath.

"No, you can't die. No, don't, not yet," Savannah cried.

Randall opened his eyes and looked at Savannah. "Oh, sweetheart, I was dying anyway."

"No, I have so many questions. This isn't fair," she said.

Touching her face, he said, "Life isn't fair, know that."

Tears dropped from her chin and landed on his cheeks.

Levi watched as father and daughter shared their last words together.

"No, please, someone help," she hollered.

"It's too late. I'm not gonna make it," he said, blood now drooling from the side of his mouth. "Do me a favor and be good to Jane, be her friend," Randall urged.

"I don't know her," Savannah said.

"Get to; she has more to teach you than I ever could," Randall said. He could feel his strength draining quickly.

"Why didn't you ever come back?" Savannah asked.

"Because that's who I was. I'm sorry...Savannah, I

gave you that name, did you know that?" Randall asked.

"No, I didn't," she said.

Jane raced into the dining hall. Seeing Randall sprawled on the floor, she went to his side. Taking his hand, she said, "My dear, you weren't supposed to leave just yet."

Randall gave Jane a sweet look and said, "Did you get your flowers?"

"I did, and I also got the package, thank you," Jane said.

"Teach her," Randall said to Jane.

"If she'll listen, I will," Jane replied, giving Savannah a gentle look.

"Come close," Randall said to Savannah.

She leaned over, her cheek close to his mouth.

"I always loved you," he said then took his last breath.

An outpouring of tears fell from Savannah's eyes.

Levi looked around the grisly scene. On the floor in front of him was the man he'd pledged to kill years ago, but who was now dead from another man's bullet. It was as if Randall was destined to die by the very tool he'd used to take so many other lives.

Clark stepped up next to Levi and said, "Well, isn't this a fine mess?"

Levi holstered his pistol and replied, "Marshal, if you won't be needing me anymore, I have somewhere to be."

"You're leaving?" Clark asked.

"Yes, I'm leaving," Levi said, removing his badge and handing it over to Clark. "Give this to Deputy Thompson. He's now the acting sheriff. I'm done."

"That's it? You're no longer sheriff?" Clark asked.

Levi wasn't trying to be heartless about what had just happened to Randall, but what more could he do? The man was dead, and there were two grieving women to attend to, but it would have to be someone else to help them. His woman was in Tucson and he needed to get there.

"No, Marshal, I'm no longer sheriff," Levi said and walked out of the hotel.

CHAPTER EIGHT

JUNE 20, 1896

TUCSON, ARIZONA TERRITORY

As he rode up close to Katherine's uncle's house, he began to regret not sending a telegram before he departed. Questions peppered his mind. Will she send me away? Should I have warned her I was coming? Will she not see me?

He let the regret simmer for a moment then let it go as fast as it had come. He was almost there, and what he had to go on was trusting the last words she'd spoken to him. She'd told him to come to Tucson when he was ready to be a proper husband and father, and he was. She would now have to trust him.

He pulled back on the reins of the horse and stopped just outside the house. As he climbed off the horse, he spotted a curtain in the front room move.

The front door opened and there stood Zeke. "Pa, you're here!" He sprinted down the brick stairs and towards Levi's open arms. When he reached him, he leapt into Levi's warm embrace and said, "I missed you so much, Pa."

Holding him tight, Levi said, "I missed you more."

"I'm so happy to see you," Zeke said.

Levi set him down and said, "I'm happy to see you. Say, where's your mother?"

"She's inside preparing dinner," Zeke said. "I'll go tell her you're here."

"No, not just yet," Levi said. "Tell me, how has your stay here been?"

"It's been good, but I've really missed you," Zeke answered.

"And how's your great-uncle doing?" Levi asked.

"He's good, a bit strict but kind," Zeke replied. "He's let me shoot almost daily."

Tousling Zeke's hair, Levi said, "Good, you should be practicing your marksmanship skills. Maybe you'll be a lawman like your father when you grow up."

"I'd love to be. I hope they still have sheriffs and deputy marshals around when I'm older," Zeke said innocently.

"Unfortunately, son, I don't think my profession will ever go away," Levi said.

"Did you capture those murderers?" Zeke asked.

"I did."

"Having us come here because of that was so scary," Zeke said.

Levi furrowed his brow and asked, "Your ma said you came here because of the murder?"

"Yes, she said it was safe here; that you thought it a

better place to be versus having us go to Prescott without you," Zeke said.

"She didn't say anything else about why you came here?" Levi asked, happy to hear his wife was keeping what had transpired between them private.

"That's what she said. Was there another reason?" Zeke asked.

"No, that was it. Say, how about we go inside; but do me a favor. Don't holler out that I'm here. I'd like to surprise her," Levi said.

"Okay."

The two went inside the house.

In the back Levi could hear the sweet sounds and melodies of Katherine singing. He leaned close to Zeke and whispered, "She seems happy."

"She is, I think," Zeke whispered back.

Levi put his index finger to his mouth, signaling for Zeke to be quiet.

Zeke nodded.

Levi tiptoed through the house until he reached the doorway to the kitchen. He peeked his head around the corner and spied Katherine rolling out a pie crust. He watched as she diligently rolled the pin back and forth, tossing more flour on top then rolling some more. He had missed her so much. Unable to wait any longer, he stepped into the kitchen. "Apple or rhubarb?"

Startled, Katherine yelped, "Levi Bass, you scared the dickens out of me. And what are you doing here?"

"Ha, ha! Pa scared you!" Zeke cackled.

"That wasn't funny. I might have hit him in the head

with this," she said, holding up the rolling pin. Wanting to talk to Levi in private, she said, "Zeke, run down to the cellar and get me several jars of stewed tomatoes. I'm going to make a sauce later for dinner."

"Okay, Ma," Zeke said and raced off.

"I didn't know you were coming. Did I miss the telegram?" she asked, wiping her flour-covered hands on her apron.

"I didn't send one," Levi replied.

"Why are you here?" she asked, feigning anger.

"You told me to come when I was ready to be a husband and father again. Well, I'm here to declare I'm ready."

"Are you?"

"I am, and I want to add that I'm deeply sorry for my behavior, and I also want to thank you," Levi confessed.

"Thank me?"

"I want to thank you for being the best wife a man could have. You not only have blessed me with Zeke, but you've been my support and have helped guide me when I go off course. I don't know what I would do without you."

"I can assume that Mr. Pritchard is still alive?" she asked.

He lowered his head and frowned. "He's not, but it wasn't by my hand. He was gunned down in the Rising Sun by men who came looking for revenge of their own."

"You had nothing to do with it?" Katherine asked.

"Katherine, you have to trust me," he said then went on to detail what had happened. He covered how he had apologized and forgiven Randall and that he came to his aid during the gunfight, but was too late.

Katherine approached him, stopping a foot away, and said, "You forgave him?"

"I did, I said it to his face, and when I did, I felt better, like a weight had been lifted," Levi said.

She took his hands, tenderly squeezed them, and said, "I'm so proud of you. That took courage and strength."

"I was only able to do it because of you, thank you," he said.

She embraced him.

The two held each other for what seemed like an eternity.

"Gross," Zeke howled upon returning to the kitchen.

Levi pulled slightly away and said, "Go get my saddlebag, and when you're done with that, take the horse to the barn and take the saddle off."

"Okay, Pa," Zeke said, running out of the kitchen.

"So what do we do now?" Katherine asked.

"Prescott, we'll head to Prescott," Levi answered.

"Prescott? I was thinking of someplace closer, like the bedroom," Katherine purred.

Levi smiled, embraced her tightly, and said, "I love you, Katherine. You've taught me a man doesn't need retribution. What he really needs is redemption."

THE END

THE RETRIBUTION OF LEVI BASS

ABOUT THE AUTHOR

G. Michael Hopf is the best-selling author of THE NEW WORLD series and other novels. He spent two decades living a life of adventure before he settled down and became a novelist full time. He is a combat veteran of the Marine Corps and a former executive protection agent. He lives with his family in San Diego, CA

Please feel free to contact him at geoff@gmichaelhopf.com with any questions or comments.

www.gmichaelhopf.com

www.facebook.com/gmichaelhopf

THE RETRIBUTION OF LEVI BASS

Books by G. MICHAEL HOPF

THE NEW WORLD SERIES
THE END
THE LONG ROAD
SANCTUARY
THE LINE OF DEPARTURE
BLOOD, SWEAT & TEARS
THE RAZOR'S EDGE
THOSE WHO REMAIN

NEW WORLD SERIES SPIN OFFS
NEMESIS: INCEPTION
EXIT

THE WANDERER SERIES
VENGEANCE ROAD
BLOOD GOLD
TORN ALLEGIANCE

THE BOUNTY HUNTER SERIES
LAST RIDE
THE LOST ONES
PRAIRIE JUSTICE

ADDITIONAL BOOKS
HOPE (CO-AUTHORED W/ A. AMERICAN)
DAY OF RECKONING
DETOUR: AN APOCALYPTIC HORROR STORY
DRIVER 8: A POST-APOCALYPTIC NOVEL
THE LAWMAN